#2

EL DIABLO
y
LOS SANTOS

By D. Patrick Carroll

D0104493

PublishAmerica
Baltimore

Softcover 9781630004453
PUBLISHED BY PUBLISHAMERICA, LLLP
www.publishamerica.com
Baltimore

Printed in the United States of America

Dedicated to:
Sylvia Richards, my best friend and confidante

Acknowledgement to:
Sergeant Jack Jackson, ret. SFPD,
Dave Armstrong, Chad Carroll

BOOK ONE

El Diablo

PART I

The Hunch

'My hunches cost me my wife, children, home, and job.'
Quote from a Gambler's Anonymous member

Chapter One

The black lab let out a yelp as the dart thumped into his behind. He whimpered as he circled, trying to extract the hard medal object lodged in his rump before he crumpled to the dirt and passed out in front of his dog house.

The man dressed in all black with a ski mask covering his face and standing atop a three step ladder, looked around for signs that someone may have been disturbed by the commotion. When he detected no lights turn on or movement coming from the house or the neighbor's homes, he stowed the dart gun in his shoulder bag and scaled the fence. His accomplice, similarly dressed, followed him.

Once they were both in the yard they crouched and ran silently to the rear of the house.

The second man held a powerful pen sized flashlight focused on the home security box, mounted on the wall. The other man removed a screwdriver from his shoulder bag and opened the cover to the home security system box. With a small pair of dikes, he stripped two sections of insulation from two wires and cross bridged them with alligator clip jumpers. He then snipped the wires. The system was now effectively disabled.

"Miguel, you are a genius," the man holding the flashlight whispered.

Miguel put his index finger to his mouth and gave his partner a disapproving look.

They crept up the stairs to the back door and Miguel attached a suction cup to a window pane. Using a bowl as a template, he scribed a circle with a diamond bladed knife.

Removing the suction cup attached to the circle of glass, he reached in and unlocked the two deadbolts and twisted the door knob.

Silently they crept through the pantry and kitchen until they came to a staircase. Ascending to the top they proceeded down a hall to an open bedroom door.

Peering in, they saw a man and a woman asleep in a king sized bed. The clock on the bed side table read 3:05 am.

Miguel produced a 22 caliper hand gun with an attached silencer from his shoulder bag while his partner unsheathed a razor sharp machete. They proceeded to either side of the bed, Miguel toward the man, who lay quietly snoring on his back. Miguel pointed his handgun between the sleeping man's eyes and nodded.

Simultaneously, he pulled the trigger and his partner placed the machete blade to the woman's throat and cupped his hand over her mouth.

"Don't say nothing, or it will be the last thing you say," the man said with a heavy Spanish accent, as the woman jerked and opened her eyes in shear panic.

They placed duct tape over her mouth and tied her with rope, spread eagle to the four bed posts. The woman laid writhing and trying in vain to scream. Tears gushed out of her eyes and down her cheeks as she lay next to her dead husband.

The two men crept out of the bedroom and down the hall, where they entered the son's bedroom. Miguel walked quickly to the sleeping boy and shot him twice in the head. The two men proceeded to the daughter's room. She was awake and frozen with fear, her blankets held tight to her neck, as the men entered.

"Don't be afraid, we will not hurt you," Miguel said, in a soothing voice.

They gagged and tied her to the bed, similar to the position they had left her mother. One hour later they exited the rear of the home and retraced their steps back to their car, parked in the alley.

"Pedro, for your first time, you did a good job," Miguel said as he started the car and sped off.

Chapter Two

Homicide Chief, San Francisco Police Department, Lieutenant John Halfhide walked out of his office and down an aisle to the cubicle of Homicide Inspectors Dwight MacArthur and Mary Dinosa. Dinosa was the only one present.

Handing her a slip of paper, he said, "You guys caught a multiple. It looks like a family of four was murdered last night or early this morning in their home out in the Avenues. Keep me posted."

Dinosa took the piece of paper, thinking what an asshole Halfhide was with his, 'keep me posted' bullshit. He sounded like a broken record. She was in a bad mood and, in general, pissed off at the opposite gender. Her boyfriend, last night had called off their relationship, spewing some crap about how they both needed their 'space'. Grabbing her hand bag and exiting the cubicle she thought, I got to stop dating fucking cops.

She passed MacArthur at the water cooler. He was chasing a pill down with a cup of water.

"Come on, Mack, we caught a multiple in the Avenues," Dinosa said, and then added, "Jesus Christ Dwight, are you still taking those magic diet pills?"

"Be glad they're not Viagra," he replied, following her to the elevator.

***

Inspectors MacArthur and Dinosa made a good homicide team. Mack had transferred from Major Crimes Detail to Homicide a little over a year ago. He was a hard nosed veteran cop with only a few months left until retirement. He was twice divorced and working on his third. He was fearful that his retirement might have to be put off so he could keep current with his alimony payments.

Dinosa was a beautiful woman in her early thirties who had served over three years in Homicide. The Brass overlooked her 'truck driver' mouth because she had a history of successful high profile felony murder arrests.

The previous year she was credited with solving the 'North Beach Killer' case and arresting the serial murderer, George Spinella, who had slain ten innocent women in the City.

Her father was a City Councilman and the family had money, lots of it. She was a trust fund baby, but liked her police work. It provided her with something to do and gave her life purpose.

Mack was the senior officer of the team, but he usually deferred to Dinosa during homicide investigations, respecting her skills and intuition. He didn't mind taking back seat, especially on the eve of his retirement. His thought was, 'why fix it if it ain't broke'.

***

Yellow crime scene tape was wrapped around temporary posts and surrounded the front of 20180 Nineteenth Avenue. Black and white cruisers were parked and blocking traffic at either end of the block. As Mary ducked under the tape she saw CSI Senior Technician Margaret Johnson starting up the front stairs of the ginger bread styled home.

"Hey Margaret, wait up will you," Dinosa yelled.

Johnson waited while Dinosa and Mack caught up to her.

"Good morning, Inspectors Dinosa and MacArthur. I heard it's a real ugly one."

"Let's find out," Dinosa replied.

When they reached the home's entrance they met two uniformed police officers. One had sergeant stripes on his sleeves.

"Sergeant Sam Woo, I haven't seen you since…?" Dinosa started to say and stopped.

"Councilwoman Nancy Bolanski's murder scene," Woo said.

Sam Woo was the Senior Field Sergeant who was one of the first responders to the crime scene of George Spinella's first and third victims. Dinosa and now retired Inspector Charles 'Chuck' Chalmers were the assigned homicide investigators.

"It's been that long? What've we got here?"

Woo referred to his notes and said, "Two patrol officers were dispatched at 1005 hours this morning to the home, after several calls were received by 911, from people voicing concern that neither Mr. John or Mrs. Clara Barnes had shown up for work this morning, nor had they answered their phones.

"After arriving and observing that the newspaper on the front walk had not been retrieved and a car was parked in the garage and no one responded to the doorbell, Officer Beane, here, retrieved an extension ladder from beside the garage and set it up to a rear window. Upon scaling the ladder and looking in the window, Officer Beane observed a naked and beheaded woman lying on a bed.

"Officer Beane immediately called for back up and a supervisor. I arrived at 1023 hours and believing it to be a just cause, I kicked in the front door. We entered and after clearing the down stairs we proceeded to the second story."

At this point Sergeant Woo, a tough veteran cop with over thirty years on the job, paused, lowered his head and mumbled, "I believe it best if you witness for yourself what we discovered upstairs. Nothing has been disturbed."

The two Inspectors and the CSI technician donned plastic suits, slip over paper shoes, plastic gloves and hair nets and entered the house, Johnson leading the way. The living room was well decorated, furnished and neat. Nothing appeared to be disturbed. They ascended the stairs located at the far corner of the room.

On the landing, in front of them, a bedroom door stood open. Inside, lying on her back in a bed, they saw a naked woman, her arms and legs tied to corresponding bed posts and her head displayed between her legs to greet any unfortunate soul who might come upon her.

They all stepped back in revulsion. MacArthur covered his mouth and, crossing himself, said, "Holy Mother of God!"

In horror of what they might now see, they walked down the hall and came to the opened door of a bathroom. Glancing in, nothing appeared to be disturbed. They continued to the next opened door. Inside, they saw the body of an adolescent boy dressed in pajamas, lying on a bed. His head was posed between his legs with two small holes between his wide opened eyes.

They proceeded to the opened door at the end of the hall. There they found the body of a naked woman lying on the bed. She was tied spread eagle with her decapitated head situated between her legs. Next to her on the floor was the beheaded body of a man, dressed in boxer shorts with his head displayed between his legs.

Upon closer inspection of the man, Johnson discovered his tongue had been cut out and it was lying on his stomach. Written in blood below his tongue was one word, 'Rata'.

"Margaret, we're going to check out the rest of the house and see if we can find a point of entry and try to figure out if there was more than one intruder. If you need us for anything, just holler. I'd appreciate if you'd look us up before you leave," Dinosa said.

"You got it," Johnson replied, and added, "It'll be a while."

Dinosa and MacArthur backed out of the room and into the hall, careful not to disturb anything. Johnson's assistant was taking pictures of the scene in the room at the end of the hall.

As they reached the bottom of the stairs, Dinosa turned and said, "Jesus Christ, Mack, I've seen some gruesome murder scenes in my time, but nothing comes close to this one."

"I have seen crime scene photos that came close. They were called 'vengaza' killings, which is Spanish for revenge. They were ordered by Latino drug lords and carried out by a gang calling themselves the 'Mexican Mafia'. They're meant to send a message to their enemies."

Dinosa picked up a family photograph from a coffee table and said, "This appears to be the people we found upstairs. It looks like the sons of bitches wiped out the entire family."

She turned to Sergeant Woo and said, "Sam, do have the names of the home's residents?"

"Yeah," Woo replied after checking his notes. "The parents are John and Clara Barnes, and according to the next door neighbor, they had two children. One is a fifteen year old girl named Tracy and the son is twelve year old Randy."

"Well, I'm going to make that the official ID on the victims, based on this picture. The Medical Examiner can confirm that later. Sergeant Woo, would you please get a hold of Community Relations and have them notify the next of kin?"

Woo nodded and pulled out his cell phone.

Dinosa and MacArthur walked through the house and stopped at the back door. A uniformed officer stood guarding against unauthorized entry to the home. He stepped aside allowing the two Inspectors to pass.

Noticing the hole in the window MacArthur said, "We know where and how the perp made entry."

They stripped themselves of the crime scene wear and proceeded down the stairs into the yard. An extension ladder was propped against the wall leading to the far corner window. What looked like an electrical box mounted on the wall next to the porch was open. After inspecting the box, MacArthur said, "I'll make sure one of Margaret's people examines and dusts this for finger prints and collects those jumper wires. This guy is one shrewd s.o.b."

In the back of the yard a black lab lay in front of his house. He tried unsuccessfully to rise as they approached. Dinosa saw the reason. She reached down and pulled the dart from his hind quarter.

"The bastard drugged him," Dinosa said.

They walked to the back fence and on tip toes, MacArthur peered over it to see the alley way behind.

"I'm gonna guess, this is where he entered the yard," MacArthur said.

"Hey Mack, give me a leg up, will ya?" Dinosa said.

"Why don't we just go back and walk around?" Mack asked.

"Just give me a hand, will ya?"

Mack bent over and cupped his hands together. Dinosa put one foot in his hands and Mack lifted. As she boosted herself over the top she lost her balance, fell and landed on her derriere on the other side of the fence.

"Mother fucker!" she exclaimed, as she quickly got up, dusting herself off.

"Don't say I didn't warn you," Mack chuckled.

"Fuck you," Dinosa replied.

She walked the alley from one of the connecting streets to the other. Returning to where Mack was on the other side of the fence, she said, "I didn't find anything, but I think you're right. This must have been his point of entry into the yard. He must have brought a ladder. I'll meet you back at the house."

She started walking down the alley as Mack started toward the house, giggling.

Mack was standing in the front yard talking to Sam Woo and two men were wheeling out a gurney with a body bag containing one of the victims, when Dinosa joined them.

"I believe there's one more body to retrieve," Woo said.

They watched as the two men placed the body bag in the back of a black moving van identified as 'San Francisco County Coroners Office'. The two men wheeled the gurney back into the house and a few minutes later emerged pushing the gurney with another body bag, followed by Margaret Johnson.

She walked over to the group and disgustedly threw her hair net and plastic gloves on the lawn.

Her hair was matted with perspiration and as she unzipped the plastic body suit and shaking her head, she said, full of vindictiveness, "That's it! I turn my retirement papers in today! I never want to go through or see anything like this again."

"I'm really sorry, Margaret. Nobody should have to see this," Mack consoled.

"Let's just catch this bastard," Dinosa contributed.

"I think you mean bastards, Mary. I found zero signs of a struggle. I think this required the efforts of more than one intruder. Someone had to subdue the wife and daughter while the other one shot the husband and boy. The coroner will have to confirm, but I believe the wife and daughter were raped," Margaret said.

"Do you have a time of death?" MacArthur asked.

"Based on liver temps, I'm going to say the two male victims were killed between 0230 and 0330 hours this morning and the two women about a half an hour later," Margaret said.

"Margaret, I'm sincerely sorry for you," Dinosa said.

"I'm serious. I'll see this one through and then I'm outta here," Margaret said, picking up her discarded clothing and walking toward her van.

***

Chapter Three

Chuck Chalmers stood on the tenth tee, waiting for the foursome in front of his to clear the fairway. He had been invited to play the prestigious Muir Woods Country Club Golf Course by his friend, Solomon Goldsmith.

His cell phone started ringing and he retrieved it from his golf bag. The caller ID told him it was his wife, Colleen.

Stepping away from the group, he said, "Excuse me guys, I have to take this."

"Hi honey, what's up?"

"Oh Chuck, Jennifer just found out Tracy Barnes and her family were murdered this morning," Colleen said with urgency. "She's taking it real hard."

"I'll be there within an hour," Chalmers said, hanging up.

Turning toward the group he exclaimed, "Sol, I'm sorry, but something has come up at home and I have to leave."

"I'm sorry, Chuck. Let me drive you back to the club house in the cart," Sol replied.

"That's okay. The parking lot is right here. I can walk, but thanks for the offer," Chalmers said, grabbing his golf bag from the cart and starting off.

"If there's anything I can do, call me," Sol yelled after him.

When he reached his car, Chalmers stowed his bag in the trunk and sitting on the rear bumper, swapped the golf shoes he was wearing for a pair of loafers.

As he drove out of the parking lot, he wondered who would murder the Barnes family. His daughter Jennifer and Tracy had been best friends since grade school. Mrs. Barnes taught Jennifer sixth grade math. They were neighbors, for Christ sake. He had never met Mr. Barnes, but recalled that he was also a school teacher. He couldn't remember the boy's name, but knew he was a few years younger than Tracy.

He drove south on Route 101 across the Golden Gate Bridge and into the City. Fortyfive minutes later he pulled into his driveway on Twenty Third Avenue. He rushed to the front door where he was greeted by Colleen.

"She's in her bedroom," Colleen said sadly.

Chalmers knocked on his daughter's door and slowly opened it. Jennifer was sitting on the edge of her bed, staring out the window, tears streaming down her cheeks. He walked over and sat gently down beside her.

She turned and wrapped her arms around him and buried her head in his shoulder and sobbed, "Oh Daddy, why?"

"Go ahead and cry, Baby."

***

"God damn it Mack, this makes no sense what so ever." Dinosa said, and then asked rhetorically, "What did any member of this family do to deserve this?"

She was back in their cubicle on the fourth floor at 850 Bryant Street, in the Homicide Detail office, sitting at her desk across from Inspector MacArthur.

Looking up, MacArthur said, "After reading Margaret's preliminary crime scene report and from what we saw, I believe this has all the ear marks of a drug related vendetta, and I'm not talking about a street hustler offing the competition. I think these ass holes hit the wrong marks."

"But this was a carefully planned operation. These guys knew what they were doing. They knew the Barnes home's layout, their alarm system, that they had a dog and that they'd all be home. Don't you think they would make sure they slaughtered the right people?" Dinosa asked.

"Hey, they may be experts at killing people, but that doesn't make them rocket scientists," Mack shrugged.

Dinosa nodded and looked down and continued reading the material in front of her. She suddenly sat up and cried, "Oh my God! This is the list of contact people provided by Community Relations. It says Jennifer Chalmers was Tracy Barnes best friend. That has to be Chuck's daughter."

She immediately picked up her phone and dialed the Chalmers' residence.

Colleen opened her daughter's bedroom door and peeked in, holding the phone receiver to her chest. She tilted her head, as if to offer an alternative, and said, "Chuck, it's Mary Dinosa."

"I'll take it," Chalmers said taking the phone and walking out of the room.

Colleen took his place beside their daughter.

"Hey Mary, how's it going?" Chalmers said.

"Oh Chuck, I'm so sorry for your family. I just found out Jenny was Tracy Barnes best friend. How is she doing?"

"She's taking it pretty hard, but she's a tough girl. Did you catch the case?"

"Yeah, me and Mack, unfortunately."

"Whatcha got?"

"Do you really want to know? It was a pretty gruesome crime scene. Actually, the worst I've ever seen."

"Your damned right I want to hear about it!"

Dinosa briefed Chalmers on the investigation, including the fact that little forensic evidence was recovered at the scene, and she spared no details in describing the crime scene. She concluded by saying, "Both Mack and I believe the perps fucked up and murdered the wrong family. We'll follow up on background checks, but so far we haven't dug up any buried bones in the Barnes' family."

"Geez Mary, they were the typical Ozzie and Harriet Nelson family. I think you guys are on the right track. Any chance we can get together after you get off tonight?"

"Sure, how about Lefty's Tavern around five?"

"You got a date," Chalmers replied.

"One more question. Who the hell are Ozzie and Harriet Nelson?"

Chalmers hung up without replying.

***

Walking into Lefty's Tavern from the bright sunshine outside, was like entering a cave. Chalmers paused for his eyes to adjust.

"Hey Chalmers, over here," he heard Dinosa yell.

He turned toward her voice and saw two silhouettes sitting at a table in the corner. He advanced slowly toward them, blinking his eyes.

When he arrived at the table, Dinosa said, "What's the matter? Having trouble adjusting the old eye balls?"

"Good to see you too, Mary, and Mack," Chalmers said taking a chair.

"Don't look so surprised, I'm part of this investigation too," Mack said.

"Jesus Mack, you're older than me and not retired yet? What, paying alimony to too many exes?" Chalmers jousted.

"In two weeks I turn in my papers," Mack replied.

"Anything new come up since we talked?" Chalmers asked.

Dinosa reached into her bag and pulled out a folder and handed it to Chalmers, saying, "These are the crime scene photos and preliminary reports. You did not get these from me. The preliminary Medical Examiners Report says he found semen in both the mother and daughter. It also indicates there were two separate donors, although the complete DNA results won't be in for a day or two."

Chalmers thumbed through the photographs, almost gagging several times. He placed them back in the folder and looked up at Mary and then at Mack. Shaking his head, he said, "No one should ever have to view these, let alone be the first ones on this crime scene."

"I got a hunch driving over here," Chalmers said and continued, "What if the perps confused the avenue with the street? Has anybody checked on who lives at the same number on Nineteenth Street?"

"Holy shit! We never thought of that." Dinosa said, sitting upright in her chair.

Mack was already on his phone.

"Yes Sergeant, this is Inspector Dwight MacArthur, Homicide. I need you to find out the names of the residents living at 20180 Nineteenth Street and anything else you can dig up on them," Mack said into his phone. There was a pause and Mack said, "I don't give a shit what time it is or how busy you are. I'm in the middle of a homicide investigation and I'd hate to hear what the Chief has to say when he learns you were too damned busy...Good, I'll hang on."

Mack cupped his hand over the receiver and said to Mary and Chuck, "It's the desk sergeant at 850 Bryant and I think I've convinced him to help us out."

"Hey Mary, who's the hunk over at the bar that hasn't kept his eyes off of you since I sat down," Chalmers said, indicating a man standing at the bar.

Mary looked over to where Chalmers indicated and said, "That could have been the next Mr. Mary Dinosa, but he blew it."

She flipped the guy the finger.

"Great," Mack said into his phone while writing in his note book.

"Bingo, we got a hit. The guy living on Nineteenth Street is married with two kids. His name is John Garcia and, get this, he works for the DEA."

"Let's go," Dinosa said, picking up her bag.

"Hey guys, I know it's probably against departmental procedure, but do you mind if I tag along?" Chalmers asked.

Dinosa looked at Mack and rolled her eyes.

"Pick up the bar tab and come along."

***

Chapter Four

Dinosa, with MacArthur in the passenger seat, pulled the unmarked sedan into a parking spot in front of 20180 Nineteenth Street. Chalmers, following behind them, made a uturn and parked on the opposite side of the street. He met them as they started up the steps to the brownstone home.

MacArthur knocked on the door. From the other side a man's voice said, "Who is it?"

Both MacArthur and Dinosa unsnapped their gun holster straps. Mack said, "It's Inspectors Mary Dinosa and Dwight MacArthur, SFPD."

The door cracked open, exposing two chain retainer locks. "Let's see some ID," the man ordered.

Mary and Mack produced and showed the man their badges. The door closed to accommodate the unlocking of the two chains and then reopened.

"Please come in. You're early," the man said.

"You were expecting us?" Mary queried.

"Weren't you dispatched to escort my family to the airport?" he asked.

"We need to talk Mr. Garcia, you are Mr. Garcia?" Dinosa asked.

"It's Agent Garcia, actually, John Garcia," the man said with a quizzical look.

He reached in the breast pocket of his sports coat and produced a DEA badge with a picture ID and showed it to them.

"We're investigating a multiple homicide," Dinosa said, and continued, "Can you tell us why you need a police detail to escort your family to the airport."

Garcia glanced curiously at Chalmers.

"This is Chuck Chalmers. He's a consultant on the case. Now, can you answer my question?"

A woman appeared in the doorway of a hall on the other side of the room. Garcia turned toward her and said, "It's okay, Donelda. Go back in the other room and stay with the kids. I'll call you when we're ready."

"Please take a seat. I don't understand. I assume you're investigating the Barnes family murder. Weren't you briefed on me and my family?" Garcia said.

"I'm afraid you're going to have to brief us, Agent Garcia," Dinosa said.

They were interrupted by a knock on the door. MacArthur went to a front window and peered out. He saw two black and white SFPD cruisers doubled parked out front and three uniformed officers standing on the side walk below the stairs to the front entrance of the house. He told the others what he saw.

"Who is it?" Dinosa asked.

"It's Officer Schmidt SFPD, Maam. We're here to escort you and your family to the San Francisco Airport."

Dinosa opened the door and was about to ask for his ID when Schmidt said, "Inspector Dinosa, what are you doing here?"

"I was going to ask you the same question," she replied.

"Beats me, my partner and I and those other two officers were detailed by our station commander to report here at 2000 hours and escort John and Donelda Garcia and their two kids to the airport," Schmidt said.

"Can you wait outside for just a minute? We'll call for you when we're ready for you," Mary said.

She closed the door and turned around, looking at Garcia she said, "I think I understand why you want to get your family to safety. Why don't you gather them up and we'll put them in one of the patrol cars for transport. You can drive with us, if you don't mind. We have some questions and you could be very helpful."

The group was about to get up from their chairs when they heard the squeal of tires and the sound of a car speeding down the street outside. Chalmers yelled, "Everybody get down," just as automatic gun fire crashed through the windows and ricocheted off of objects and walls in the room.

With the exception of several single rounds being fired outside, the shooting stopped.

Mack yelled, "Is everybody okay?"

Garcia was running toward the back of the house calling for his wife and family. He found them huddled together in the corner of the kitchen.

Relieved, Garcia said, "Are you okay?"

"I think so," his wife trembled.

In the front room, Dinosa crouched down, opened the door and crept out onto the porch. MacArthur was right behind her. The scene was chaotic. Officer Schmidt was cradling another officer on the sidewalk below the stairs, waving and yelling at the other two officers, "Go, Go, Go!"

The two officers jumped into their cruiser and with lights flashing and siren blaring sped off.

Schmidt spoke excitedly into his shoulder radio, "Shots fired, officer down at 20180 Nineteenth Street. Officers in pursuit of a sixties model, dark Chevrolet Impala, last seen headed west on Nineteenth Street!"

He looked down at the man cradled in his arms. The man's eyes were barely open and he was gushing blood from the side of his forehead. Placing a hand on the wound, to help stem the flow of blood, Schmidt said, "Hang in their kid. The ambulance is on the way."

MacArthur tapped Dinosa on the shoulder and said, "Mary, why don't you go back inside and tend to the Garcia family? I'll take care of things out here."

She nodded and holstering her weapon, walked back into the house. She found Chalmers and the Garcia family sitting at the kitchen table.

"What's the scene like outside?" Chalmers asked.

"Not good," Dinosa said, wiping the sweat off her brow. "We've got an officer down and a squad car in pursuit. MacArthur and Schmidt are with the wounded officer. It doesn't look good."

Multiple sirens could be heard in the distance and were getting louder. Chalmers and Dinosa walked back out to the front porch. An ambulance was parked on the street and two EMTs were working on the wounded officer. Three or four other police squad cars were parked at angles in the street.

"Jesus Christ, Chuck, this is a war," Dinosa said.

"I'd say this was just a battle. I'm afraid the war was declared some time ago," Chalmers sighed.

Hey watched as a black limousine turned the corner onto Nineteenth Street and wind its' way through the parked squad cars. It stopped behind the ambulance and a uniformed officer got out of the passenger side and opened the rear door. Assistant Deputy Chief Madelyn Keene stepped out.

"Ah shit! This is all we need." Dinosa moaned.

"I'm out of here. Put in a good word for me to Garcia, will you? I'll call you later," Chalmers said and disappeared into the house.

He walked back to the kitchen and asked Garcia if he could have a moment with him. The two stepped into the hallway and Chalmers handed Garcia a slip of paper with his name and phone number on it and said, "Agent Garcia, I'm a retired SFPD Homicide Inspector. I have some, what could be called, unusual resources and I'd like to help you and your family."

Garcia looked at him curiously and said, "I don't understand."

"Talk to Inspector Dinosa. Is there a back way out of here?"

"Yes, you can go out of that door at the end of the hall and down the stairs. You can leave through the side gate on the far side of the garage."

"Thanks, and please call me."

Chalmers exited the home and as he opened the gate next to the garage he glanced up at the front porch and caught Dinosa's eye. Deputy Chief Keene's back was toward him and Dinosa quickly ushered her into the house.

Walking directly toward the group of cops, now gathered in front of the house, he ignored MacArthur and said, "Hey, Schmidtie, what's going on."

"Inspector Chalmers, what the hell are you doing here?"

"It's retired Inspector Chuck now. I was just visiting a friend down the street when the shit started. You got an officer down? How's he doing?"

"They're working on him, but I don't think he's gonna make it. His name's Timothy Cook. He was a rookie and I was his training officer. He's only been on the force for a week."

"Ah shit, did you get the shooter?" Chalmers asked sincerely.

"Actually it was shooters, a drive by. We just heard pursuit chased them up Twin Peaks at high speeds. The dumb bastards didn't make a turn and they said the car flipped five or six times before it hit the bottom. All three Hispanic occupants were declared dead at the scene. The sons of bitches are probably better off that way."

"If the kid doesn't make it, will you let me know? I'd like to make it to the memorial."

Chalmers paused, and then added, "Hey, do you think you could have some of the guys clear a path for me? I'm parked across the street there."

"You got it," Schmidt replied.

Chapter Five

When Chalmers got home, the house was dark and he checked on his sleeping wife and daughter. He walked out onto the back deck to make his calls.

"Hello Sean, this is Chuck. Sorry to call so late, but it's urgent."

"No need to apologize, Chuck, you should know you can call anytime. What's up?"

"I think I've found a worthy cause for the foundation we set up."

"Does it have anything to do with the Barnes family massacre?" Sean guessed.

"Yep," Chalmers said, not really surprised.

"I thought you'd never call. What've you got?"

"I should have enough to present it to the board by tomorrow night."

"Great, I'll call for a meeting. How does eight o'clock at my place sound?"

"Sounds good, I'll see you then, and thanks."

After hanging up, Chalmers called Dinosa.

"Hey Mary, what's up?"

"Jesus Christ, Chalmers, you and your hunches. Do me a favor and call someone else the next time you get one. They seem to complicate my life, but I guess, in a good way. Shit, did I just say that? I'm almost afraid to ask, what do you need?"

"Well, first you can fill me in to what happened after I left the Garcia place."

"Can you believe that asshole Jack Jackson, from the FBI showed up with a couple of his ass lickers? Said he was instructed to take over the drive by investigation, seeing how a federal agent had been attacked.

"I told him he could go fuck himself, but that ankle Keene capitulated. Can you believe it?"

Chalmers remembered Dinosa's use of the word 'ankle' was her polite way for calling someone the 'C' word, but anatomically speaking it was two and a half feet lower.

"Yeah, I can believe it. I suppose the feds took the Garcia family under protective custody?" Chalmers asked.

"You suppose right, but to answer your next question, yes we did get a little info out of Garcia before Jackson showed up.

"It seems Garcia was the FAST leader of an operation called 'Thunder and Lightning'.

The team was responsible for making the largest cocaine bust is U.S. history, over half a billion dollars."

"Whoa, Mary, you're going too fast. First, what the hell is fast?" Chalmers asked.

"Oh sorry, I didn't know either. FAST is a DEA acronym for 'Foreigndeployed Advisory and Support Team'. They're composed of seven man teams trained in small unit tactics and close quarter battle. When invited by the host country, they are authorized to go on foreign soil to fight the war on drugs.

"Anyway, Garcia says operation 'Thunder and Lightning' targeted the Vasquez drug cartel in Mexico. He says their reputation for violence is legendary. They've been know to wipe out entire villages if there's only a hint of a problem. Their signature is to behead their victims.

"They are becoming more brazen. Garcia believes his family was targeted to send a message to the United States that they are prepared for war.

"That's when 'Action Jackson' showed up."

"Did Garcia ask about me?" Chalmers inquired.

"Yes he did. He said you gave him your phone number and told him you said you could help him and his family and asked me what I thought. I told him what I knew, which by the way is very little, about your involvement with the George Spinella capture. He seemed to know more about that than I do."

"One more question, do you know where the FBI took them?" Chalmers asked.

"Sorry, I don't have a clue," Dinosa replied.

"Thank you," Chalmers said and hung up.

***

Chalmers rolled over and looked at the bedside clock. It said 7:05 am. He pushed off the covers and sat up on the side of his bed. His thoughts were of yesterday's events. What started out as a beautiful morning on the golf course with friends had ended as a nightmare.

He dropped to his knees and then to the prone position. He pumped out twenty pushups and then rolled over and did twenty situps. He got to his feet a little out of breath and walked to the master bathroom, scratching his balls. He looked in the mirror above the sink, sucked in his stomach and flexed. Not bad for fiftythree, or was it fiftyfour, he thought.

He showered, shaved and dressed and went out to the kitchen. His daughter was sitting at the breakfast table, playing with her bowl of cereal. Her cheeks were flushed and her eyes swollen.

Colleen was placing a plate of eggs, toast and link sausage at his place. He walked up behind her and kissed her on the neck and said, "Good morning, family," and then added, "Honey, I was thinking I've put on a few pounds since retirement and maybe I ought to cut out the sausage."

"Fine," Colleen said, reaching for the three sausages.

Chalmers, playfully pulled away the plate and said, "Maybe we can start that program tomorrow. I mean, you already cooked these."

"Only two more days of school until summer break. What are your plans for the summer break?" Chalmers said to Jennifer, trying to sound cheerful.

"Pop, tomorrow they're having a memorial for Tracy in the school auditorium and they've asked me to say something. I don't think I can do it," she said, looking down, still fiddling with the spoon in her bowl of cereal.

"Do you want to talk about it?" he asked.

"What could I say?" she mumbled.

"Well, what did she mean to you?" he asked.

"She was everything to me. She was always there when I needed her. She was strong and brought out and saw the best in everyone. She was brave, like the day in the fifth grade when she stood up to Johnnie Crabtree when he was picking on her little brother."

"What was it about her that you'll never forget?"

"Oh Pop, there's so many things about her I will never, ever forget. Like the time we had an argument and didn't talk to each other for a whole day. She called me that night and apologized when actually the fight was my fault.

"And then there's the time when she made the freshman cheerleading squad and I didn't and she saw how hurt I was.

She actually said she would quit. That was so nice of her. I told her it was totally dumb, but if I would have let her, I honestly think she would have.

"She was my best friend and I loved her so much."

"I think you just said what you can say tomorrow," Chalmers said.

Jennifer rose from the table and walked around to her Dad and putting her arms around him, sighed and said, "Thank you, Daddy."

She grabbed her back pack and after kissing her mother left out the back door for school.

Colleen came from behind the counter, leaned over, kissed him on the ear and whispered, "You're a great Daddy."

He heard his cell phone that he'd left in the bedroom, ring. Getting up he said, "We'll resume this conversation later," and hustled off.

"Mr. Chalmers, it's John Garcia," The voice on the other end said.

"Please call me Chuck. I'm glad you called. What can I do for you?"

"Last night you said you had resources and you could help me. Exactly, what did you mean?"

"Before I answer that, I need to ask you a few questions," Chalmers said.

When there was no reply, Chalmers continued, "First, are you calling me from a safe line?"

"Yes, I ditched my custodian and I'm calling from a pay phone," he replied.

"Good. Inspector Dinosa told me you thought your family was targeted because of your involvement in a recent operation. Do you know why?"

"I don't know. I operated in the field. It's a good chance I got made," Garcia replied.

"Have you considered you may have a leak in your agency?"

Garcia pondered that thought. When he didn't answer, Chalmers asked, "John, are you still there?"

"Yes," Garcia answered and continued, "That's a possibility."

"Would you have someone in mind?"

"Hell, if it were an inside mole, it could be any of ten or twenty people, maybe more."

"Who did you call when you discovered you and your family were targeted?"

"I called my supervisor in Arlington, Virginia. His name is Luke Watson. He's the Special Ops Administrator in our home office. He told me to sit tight and he would get back to me. He called back in ten minutes and said he'd arranged for an SFPD escort for me and my family to transport us to the SFO for a chartered flight back to Arlington. I assumed they would put us up in a safe house."

"Without telling me where, are you still in the Bay Area?"

"Yes," Garcia said.

"Do you think you could get away around 8:30 tonight to make another phone call?"

"I think I can manage that."

"Good, write down this number," Chalmers said and he gave him Sean O'Farrell's private listing.

"If you can call that number tonight, I will answer your questions," Chalmers said.

Chalmers left for Sean O'Farrell's home in the Sausalito Hills home at 7:00 pm. Fifty minutes later he pulled up to the O'Farrell Estate and stopped at the entrance gate. Before he could push the button on the intercom, the gate swung open.

He drove up the tree lined lane and around a sweeping curve, revealing a large brownstone mansion. The lane ended at a circle driveway where he saw Sean at the top of the stairs on the front door landing, waving him up.

Sean O'Farrell was the descendant of a long line of San Francisco blue bloods. The first O'Farrell arrived in San Francisco in the eighteen forties, an Irish immigrant. He opened a mercantile business catering to gold miners and pioneers. Over the years the family had invested in businesses and real estate in the area and prospered very well.

Sean and the other men he was about to meet had several things in common. They were successful billionaires and they all had a beloved family member murdered by the same serial killer, George Spinella, a little over two years ago.

Retired Homicide Inspector Chuck Chalmers was hired by this group and solved the case and helped bring the murderer to justice. He was also richly rewarded for his efforts.

Reaching the landing, Chalmers extended his hand and said, "How are you Sean. Good to see you."

"It's good to see you too, Chuck. Come on in, the others are here and waiting in the den."

When they entered the den, Chalmers saw the other three members of the foundation's board of director's were present. Sol Goldsmith, George Armstrong and Sean's son, Ian, all rose to greet him.

Sol Goldsmith was the husband of Spinella's first victim. He was in the import business. His company owned the exclusive rights to import and distribute several popular German and Mexican beers in the U.S.

George Armstrong's mother was Spinella's fifth victim. He was a criminal lawyer and one of the heirs to the vast Armstrong publishing company fortune.

Ian Armstrong was Sean's son and business partner. He had resigned his commission in the Navy after his mother was murdered by the same man. She was Spinella's fifth, of ten total victims slain in San Francisco within a two week period.

Chalmers took an empty chair and began, "I assume Sean has told you that I'm here to discuss the murder of the Barnes family yesterday morning.

"I've seen the crime scene photos. Gentlemen, this was not just the murder of four people. It was the most brutal and savage slaughter I have ever seen. The victims were beheaded and Mrs. Barnes and her fifteen year old daughter, Tracy, were raped.

And their only crime was to be living on Nineteenth Avenue instead of Nineteenth Street."

He went on to tell the group about the address foul up and who the intended victims were.

He told them about the drive by shooting at the Garcia home the night before and the ensuing events. He also explained that John Garcia was a DEA agent and about his recent involvement with busting a large shipment made by the Vasquez drug cartel.

"My proposal is this; we use our resources to find the bastards that perpetrated this crime and the ones that ordered it, and hurt them bad."

Chalmers concluded by saying, "I must tell you all, I have a personal agenda in this. Tracy Barnes was my daughter's best friend and I'll pursue this with or without your help."

"Is this Vasquez the same man that acted as my accommodator in Mexico?" Goldsmith asked.

"I think so; it's too much of a coincidence. We should get some answers soon. I've asked John Garcia to call us here tonight," Chalmers replied, and checking his wrist watch added, "In about five minutes."

The 'accommodator' Goldsmith had referred to was a cost of doing business in Mexico. A company he had hired called 'Los Exporta' received a two percent commission on the price of the goods he purchased in Mexico. He considered it legal graft, but a necessary expense for doing business in Mexico. When he learned 'Los Exporta' had ties to the Vasquez drug cartel and was being investigated by the FBI, he severed his agreement and found another 'accommodator'.

"I'm inclined to vote yes, but I'd like to hear what this Garcia has to say before I commit," George Armstrong said.

The phone located on top of the bar counter in one corner of the room rang. Sean answered and carrying it back to the center of the room said, "Hello Agent Garcia, glad you called. I'm going to put you on speaker."

He laid the phone down on top of a coffee table.

"Hello John, this is Chuck Chambers. How are you and your family doing?"

"I guess we're okay, but I'm confused."

"Let me try to explain," Chalmers said.

"First, Inspector Dinosa told me you knew something about the capture of George Spinella. What do you know?"

"All I know is the scuttle butt I heard out of Arlington. The word was, you were involved with some kind of a civilian commando outfit that kidnapped Spinella from a Venezuelan Island and brought him in. The consensus was, it was a job well done and the less we knew about the better," Garcia said.

Chalmers glanced around the room at the men, nodding their approval.

He said, "I want you to know, I am presently in the same room with the men that financed that operation and the man that planned and pulled it off.

"We have an interest in helping you to keep your family safe and also avenging the slaughter of the Barnes family, but we need your help. Are you willing?"

Garcia replied, "I've been thinking about what you said about the possibility of there being an inside leak or mole within the DEA. I'm afraid you might be right, which puts my family at risk even as we talk."

Ian O'Farrell interrupted and said, "Where are you being kept and who and how many people are guarding you?"

Chalmers added, "You're now talking to the man who planned and executed the Spinella operation."

"As far as I know, we only have two FBI agents with us. I don't believe they missed me when I called you earlier, Chuck, but I'm sure they're missing me now. I didn't observe anyone stationed on the street outside of the house they're keeping us in, but that doesn't mean there isn't any.

"We're being kept in a safe house in the Piedmont hills. The address is 386 Robertson Court, off of Joaquin Miller Road. The home is fairly secluded."

Ian said, "John, we're going to put you on hold for just a minute, please stay on."

He looked at his father and asked, "What do you think, Dad?"

Sean nodded approval and Ian picked back up, "John, we think we can provide better security for you and your family. Are you up for that?"

"You bet, what do you propose?"

***

Chapter Six

"You stupid, stupid assholes!" Pablo Vasquez screamed in Spanish into the phone. "How could you allow this to happen?!" he demanded.

"Pedro was supposed to locate the home and then I did all the planning. The family fit the description we were given and the operation went off like clock work," Miguel answered defensively.

"Like clockwork? You slaughtered the wrong family you assholes," Vasquez yelled and continued, "And what's with this driveby shooting. Who the hell authorized that fucking fiasco?"

"We had nothing to do with that. It must have been ordered by Hector Ramirez, trying to get in your favor," Miguel replied.

"Where are you now?" Vasquez demanded.

"We're still in San Francisco at the safe house. What are your orders?" Miguel said meekly.

"Just stay put and I'll get back to you and don't do anything stupid, please," Vasquez said sarcastically.

***

Chalmers pulled the luxury van off the road and parked under an oak tree between two of the large homes nestled in the hills of Piedmont. He looked at his watch which read 2:03 am.

Ian, dressed in dark clothing and carrying a shoulder nap sack, instructed him to wait there and disappeared out of the passenger side door. He crept around the oak tree and through an open field about twenty yards wide until he came to a back yard fence. He scaled the fence and quietly ran to the back corner of the house.

According to the plan he and Garcia had made earlier, he placed a dog whistle to his lips and blew hard. The whistle was tuned to produce a frequency that could not be detected by human ears.

In an upstairs bedroom of the house, Boink, the family's six year old Jack Russell dog, perked up his ears. Ian blue into the whistle again. Boink jumped off the bed and began barking ferociously.

There was an immediate tap on the bedroom door that was occupied by John and Donelda Garcia and their dog, followed by a man's voice that asked, "Is everything okay in there?"

"I think I just heard a noise out front under our window," Garcia said.

The man outside the door raced back to the top of the staircase and yelled down, "Hey Frank, we heard a noise out front. Check it out."

Garcia exited the bedroom and walked down the hall and stood behind the FBI agent. The agent turned his head and started to say, "Mr. Garcia, you should go back…"

Garcia reached out and grasped the agent's neck in the crook of his arm and applied a nonlethal choke hold he had learned in his 'FAST' training. Garcia was much larger than the agent and he easily over powered him. Within ten seconds the agent went limp and Garcia dropped him gently to the carpet.

He motioned Donelda, who was holding Boink, to follow him. They entered the corner bedroom where his eight and ten year old boys were. He knew he had less than three minutes before the agent would come to and he hoped the other agent would be kept busy out front for at least that long.

He ran to the rear window and removed the pane of glass that he had earlier that evening dislodged from its' frame. From down below, Ian lobbed a rope ladder up and Garcia grabbed it on the first attempt. He attached the grappling hooks under the window sill and helped his children out of the window and onto the ladder. He then threw the two bags that contained a few personal possessions the family was able to gather the night before, out of the window. He helped his twelve year old out and onto the ladder and then his eight year old. He grabbed Boink from his wife and helped her up and out. Holding the dog under one arm, he followed.

Safely on the ground, Ian gave the rope ladder a whip and it came tumbling down. He gathered it up and stowed it in his nap pack and motioned the family to follow him to the fence.

There, Ian motioned for Garcia to scale the fence and then one by one gave a leg up to the rest of the family, with Garcia on the other side to help them down. He scaled the fence and they followed him, running across the field.

As they neared the large oak tree they heard someone bellow, "Son of a bitch!"

Ian turned and saw a man glaring out of the upstairs window.

The group reached the van and piled in. Chalmers started the engine and they began the hour and a half trip back to the O'Farrell estate.

***

Waiting to meet the van as it pulled into the circular driveway below the O'Farrell home was a group of three people. Sean O'Farrell was flanked by a pretty woman in her mid thirties on one side and a large black man on the other.

Chalmers recognized the large man. He knew him as Grant, a member of the team that brought Spinella to justice. Grant was a friend of Ian's, and a former mate in the U.S. Navy Seals. He was a large muscular black man who had proved himself in many battles.

Chalmers later came to find out the woman's name was Sheila Lamont, the oldest daughter of Sean O'Farrell. Her husband was a member of the U.S. Army's Special Forces and was killed in Afghanistan, leaving her widowed at the time with an eleven year old son and a ten year old daughter. Sheila and her children moved into the mansion shortly after her mother's untimely death two years ago and assumed the role of family matriarch.

After a brief greeting and introductions made, Sheila hugged Donelda and said, "You must be exhausted. Please come along and we'll get you and your family settled."

Chalmers said good night and told Sean he would call later that day. He walked to his car and began the drive home.

The group proceeded up the stairs and into the home. In the foyer, Sean said, "John, welcome to my house. Why don't you and your family get a good nights' sleep and we'll talk later?"

***

When Chalmers got home he found Colleen, dressed in her night gown, curled up asleep on the couch in the living room. Under a reading lamp with a book lying next to her, he couldn't help but pause and realize what a lucky man he was to have her in his life.

He shook her gently and said, "Hey Pooch, goin' my way?"

She opened her eyes and smiled and then reached up and kissing him, pulled him down on top of her and said, "Sailor, wherever you go is my way."

"How's Jennifer doing?" he asked, trying to make himself comfortable on the narrow sofa.

"She's doing fine. When she got home from school, she went right to the computer and started working on what she would say tomorrow, or I mean today, at Tracy's memorial service."

"Honey, I'm afraid I did it again. I've screwed up our retirement plans again," Chalmers said.

"If it has anything about getting justice for the Barnes family, you haven't screwed up anything."

She glanced at the clock and said in mock horror, "My God, does that say it's five am," and then added, "Hey sailor, how about a little hubbahubba?"

"Aye, aye, ma'am, you're on," he replied, beaming.

They got off the couch and walked hand in hand back to their bedroom. 'Hubbahubba' was their pet way of saying 'let's make love'.

***

Chapter Seven

Chalmers rolled over in bed and looked at the clock beside him. It read 11:00 am. "Oh, shit!" he exclaimed, throwing off the covers and rushing out the door and down the hall into the kitchen.

"Good morning, glory," Colleen said, pouring a cup of coffee.

She was wearing a knee length black slip and dark panty hose.

"I was just about ready to come in and wake you. You have time for a quick shower and shave before the memorial starts at noon," she said, handing him a cup of coffee, and then added, "I picked up some oat bran muffins in lieu of bacon and eggs for your breakfast."

Back in the bedroom, he picked up his cell phone and dialed the O'Farrell home.

"Hello Sean, it's Chuck. I'm afraid I can't get there for a couple of hours. It's Tracy Barnes memorial."

"Don't worry," Sean said and continued, "The Garcia's aren't even up yet. We'll hold off our talk until you get here."

"Thanks," Chalmers replied and hung up.

When they arrived at Jennifer's school the parking lot was full and they had to park on the street and ran to the school auditorium. Entering through a door at the back of the auditorium, they realized they were late. There was standing room only behind the chairs on the gymnasium floor.

Jennifer was sitting in a row of chairs occupied by other students and teachers on a stage at the front of the room. As they made their way to the standing area, Chalmers waved at her and was acknowledged with a nod.

When it came time for Jennifer to talk, she strode stridently to the podium.

She began, "I ask myself why my best friend, Tray Barnes had to die. Some of you know my father was a San Francisco police officer and he saw a lot of death doing his job. When I asked him, he told me we will never know why a person had to die. He said the question should be, why did they live?

"Here is why, I think Tracy lived..."

When Jennifer finished her eulogy, Chalmers felt a tremendous sense of pride and was glad he had donned a pair of sun glasses when he left the house.

Chapter Eight

Chalmers was greeted by a man even larger than Grant when he pulled up and parked below the O'Farrell home. The man wore khaki knee length shorts and a white tee shirt that revealed bulging muscles and very little body fat. His hair was cropped short and Chalmers wondered if he was another one of Ian's Seal friends.

The man approached the six foot, two inch Chalmers and towered over him. He extended his hand and said, "You must be Mr. Chalmers. Hi, my name is Jeremy Colt."

Chalmers winced in anticipation of pain as he extended his hand, but was pleasantly surprised when the man's grip was firm, but gentle.

"Nice to meet you, Mr. Colt," Chalmers said, looking up at him.

"Everyone's at the pool behind the house, come on."

Chalmers followed Colt. They bypassed the steps to the home's entrance and walked up a white pebbled path that wound up the hill and around the house. The path followed a six foot, well trimmed hedge on the outside and multi colored tulips lined the other side. It ended behind the house at steps that led to a sprawling redwood deck that surrounded a large kidney shaped swimming pool.

A net extended across the pool and the Garcia boys, John Jr. and Robert, Sheila's son Matt, and Grant were playing pool volleyball. Donelda, Sheila and her daughter Shannon were sun bathing and chatting, laying on lounges next to the pool.

Garcia, Sean and Ian sat around a patio table underneath an awning that extended from the rear of the house.

"Good morning Chuck, pull up a chair," Sean said, pouring from a pitcher of iced tea into a glass and handing it to him.

Sean continued, "John here was just starting to tell us about operation 'Thunder and Lightning'. Why don't you continue, John?"

"Pablo Vasquez is a Mexican citizen who owns and resides on a ten thousand acre ranch bordering Lake Chapala, Mexico, about twentyfive miles southeast of Guadalajara.

Senor Vasquez had been on the DEA's radar for over ten years.

"He started out as an enforcer in the Medeline drug cartel, about twentyfive years ago, when he was sixteen years old. Over the years he rose to be one of Pablo Escobar's top lieutenants. He was Escobar's most reliable assassin and became infamous for decapitating his victims.

"Vasquez became a trusted associate of Escobar, but as it turned out that trust was misplaced. Vasquez was an ambitious man, and it was his tip to Interpol that led the Columbian Police to Escobar's hideout in Medeline, Columbia, where he was shot to death in December, 1993.

"It took Vasquez almost fifteen years to rise to the top of the cartel. He slaughtered literally thousands of people he believed to be in his way. By 2008 he had eliminated virtually all of his competition and now we believe he controls over ninety percent of the cocaine coming out of Columbia and Bolivia, and the majority of marijuana shipments from Mexico. He has changed the name from the 'Medeline Cartel' to simply 'El Diablo', the devil.

Garcia continued, "His main distribution in the United States is made through a ruthless gang called 'The Mexican Mafia'. They usually take possession of the drugs on this side of the border. They have an elaborate distribution system throughout the U.S. Their honcho is a man named Eric Morales who, ironically, happens to be a brotherinlaw of Pablo Vasquez, and lives outside of Phoenix, Arizona.

"Operation 'Thunder and Lightning' was planned by our Operations Administration in Arlington, Virginia, about two months ago. The idea was to badly damage 'El Diablo's operation and hopefully lead to the arrest of Eric Morales and some of his top lieutenants.

"My FAST people working out of the San Francisco DEA office were assigned to put boots on the ground in Mexico and follow shipments to the United States. Intel gathered by our agency and the CIA told us a large shipment of cocaine was due to leave Guadalajara within two weeks. It was being amassed in a warehouse there."

Garcia was interrupted by Sheila who had walked up from her pool side perch accompanied by Shannon and Donelda.

"We're going in to work out in the gym. How many people should I expect for supper?" She asked.

Sean looked questioningly at Chalmers who said, "Oh, no thank you Sheila. I have plans with my family."

"Well then, I guess you can just count the heads that are here," Sean said.

The women disappeared into the house.

Sean looked at Garcia and said, "Please continue."

"Let's see, where was I? Oh yeah, the warehouse in Guadalajara. My team and I already had it under twentyfour seven surveillance. For the five days we observed a van arriving and off loading its' cargo two to three times a day.

"We followed one of the vans as it left and it led us back to the Vasquez villa and compound. The place was almost impregnable and I thought it too dangerous to breach. I stationed a couple of agents there to observe. They reported back that a twin engine airplane was landing on a private strip on the ranch almost daily. The plane's point of origin was traced back to a private strip outside of Bogotá, Columbia.

"After a week we observed a tractor trailer pull up to the warehouse and begin loading. The next day it departed and we followed it west to Puerto Vallarta. There it was loaded onto a deluxe commercial cruise ship call the 'Caribbean Princess'. We found out the ship had departed Miami twenty days earlier for a cruise that would end in five days at the Port Of San Diego.

"My team was ordered to San Diego and told to hook up with agents there. When the 'Caribbean Princess' docked we observed the subject cargo as it was loaded into another tractor trailer. As they were unloading the ship's hold, we watched as a U.S. customs official approached one of the men supervising the transfer of cargo. He was handed an envelope and promptly departed. This all took place in broad daylight.

"We tailed the semi all the way to the warehouse in Barstow, California, where we made the bust. To our surprise, Eric Morales was waiting to meet the truck. I was given the unfortunate task of cuffing him.

"We took down about eight others, two of whom were high level figures in 'The Mexican Mafia'. The raid resulted in the confiscation of a street value of about a half of a billion dollars worth of cocaine."

Chalmers whistled and said, "My math isn't that great, but I calculate that's got to be over a ton of cocaine."

Garcia nodded.

"The Mexican government has to know this is going on. Why don't they do something?" Sean asked, amazed.

"Well, you saw how easy it was to get that stuff through our customs. It's no different, actually worse in Mexico. The 'El Diablo' cartel ships over one hundred billion dollars of illegal drugs into this country every year, and at least that much to the rest of the world. Less than one percent of those drugs are confiscated by the DEA or other law enforcement agencies. Hell, payoffs to official authorities are just a small cost of doing business," Garcia shrugged.

"I think we know now why you were targeted with this 'vengaza', but how did they know about you're involvement," Chalmers asked.

"It almost had to be an internal leak, "Garcia said and continued, "Ten years ago, when I joined the DEA, there was a real feeling within the field agents that we were making a difference. Since then, morale has drastically declined.

"We feel the present Administration and Justice Department doesn't give a shit. They seem to be more interested in protecting their own asses and fighting individual States rather than fighting the war on drugs. Maybe it's payoff money. I don't know.

"Given that state and the lure of big money, I can see where one or more of my associates might turn. I just wish I knew who the son of a bitch is."

Sean crinkled his eye brows in thought and then asked, "If there is a leak in your agency, why didn't they tip Vasquez off to operation 'Thunder and Lightning'?"

"I've given that a lot of thought and I have no answer. When we can answer that, we'll know who the leak is," Garcia replied.

Chalmers looked at his watch and said, "Gentlemen, I'm sorry, but I have to leave. Can we take this up again tomorrow morning?"

"Of course, how about we meet here at nine am?" Sean said.

After Chalmers left, Garcia said, "Can I ask what your intentions are, exactly?"

Ian replied, "Well, I can tell you our intentions are to do more than just hurt Pablo Vasquez and his 'El Diablo' cartel."

Garcia leaned back in his chair and folded his arms and said, "What happened to the Barnes family should've happened to my family and I feel partially responsible. Yesterday I turned in my resignation to the Drug Enforcement Administration."

Before he could be interrupted, he leaned forward and continued, "I don't have any resources and I'm certainly not a Navy Seal or Army Green Beret, but I have had extensive training in small arms and hand to hand combat. I also have a lot of knowledge of 'El Dorado' and Pablo Vasquez and his operation.

"I believe I can make a contribution to your group and I'm asking to be a member of your mission," Garcia said, first looking at Ian and then Sean.

"Let me tell you a little about our 'group'," Ian said, glancing at his father.

After receiving a nod, he continued, "I recruited active duty Navy Seals who were members of my team before I resigned my commission to participate in an illegal act of revenge. I put their lives and careers in jeopardy, but they committed themselves and we avenged the senseless murder of my father's wife and my mother plus the murders of nine other innocent women.

"We recruited retired Homicide Inspector Chuck Chalmers because of his knowledge of the ass hole we were after and because of his access to SFPD intel.

"We were all united because we wanted to right a wrong. My father and some of the other victim's family felt the same way and financed our operation. They subsequently formed the 'Justice Foundation' which serves one purpose, to right a wrong.

"Avenging the slaughter of the Barnes family will be our first mission. We are dedicated to see that the people responsible are brought to justice by any means. This will be an illegal enterprise from start to finish. Are you prepared to make that same commitment?"

"Yes, I am."

"Then welcome aboard, John Garcia," Sean said.

***

Chapter Ten

Chalmers pulled into his driveway, mentally exhausted from the day's events. Jennifer was with a group of her friends in the front yard. They were hugging each other and it appeared saying their goodbyes. He parked in the detached garage and took the back stairs to his deck and entered the house.

Colleen was busy picking up dishware from the dining room table when he entered.

"Training for your next career?" Chalmers said, trying to be funny.

"Yes, and I've just been promoted to boss. Get in the kitchen and start washing the dishes."

"Yes, ma'am," he said, walking past her and patting her on the rear on his way to the kitchen.

"We will not tolerate sexual harassment in this work place," she exclaimed in mock indignation.

He washed as she dried the dishes. He started the conversation by saying, "What would you say if I were to go on a trip soon?"

"Oh, I don't know. How long would you be gone?"

"It's hard to say, maybe a couple of weeks."

Colleen laid her towel on the counter top and looked sternly at her husband.

"For thirty years I've watched you leave this house every day, not knowing for sure if you'd be coming home that night. I think I've done a pretty good job of not dwelling on that thought. Don't you think it's time for both of us to relax and enjoy what time we have left?" She said, trying to remain calm.

"Even if that means turning a blind eye to the senseless slaughter of our neighbors and Jessica's best friend when I know I can make a difference?" Chalmers replied, attempting to sound reasonable.

"You and your, your...goddamned Lone Ranger complex!" she cried, tearing off her apron and throwing it on the kitchen table and dashing out of the room.

"Ah, shit," he moaned to himself, feeling like the most ungrateful bastard in the world.

He followed her path and found her lying on their bed, her head buried in the pillow, sobbing quietly.

He sat down on the bed next to her and gently put his hand on her back and said, consolingly, "I'm sorry, Babe. You're right. I'm being selfish, again. Can you forgive me?"

She sat up on the bed and gently placed her palm on his cheek and sighed, "Oh Chuck, why should it stop now? Of course you have to do this, and we'll be fine."

After dinner Chalmers picked up the cordless home phone and walked out onto the deck and noticed Colleen had turned on the hot tub. This night might turn out okay after all, he thought and dialed Dinosa's number.

"Hey Mary, it's Chuck."

"You know, Chalmers, and I prefer it when you call me Dinosa. Whatdya' need?"

"Come on, Dinosa, you know what I need."

"Well, we entered the two DNA results in the national data base and got zero hits. We believe they are probably foreign nationals. The three pukes we found at the bottom of Twin Peaks were all Hispanic and belonged to the street gang, 'The Mexican Mafia'.

"Based on cell phone records, we believe the drive by was ordered by Hector Ramirez, el president of the gang's Bay Area Chapter. Unfortunately, phone records aren't enough to charge the bastard.

"Since the feds took over the investigation, we've been ordered to stand down. The scuttle butt says the feds fucked up big time and lost the Garcia family. You wouldn't know their whereabouts, would you?"

"No comment," Chalmers said.

"Of course you don't," she chuckled.

"Can you tell me where to find this, Hector Ramirez?"

"Here we go again. I give you my virtue and you give me a limp dick."

Chalmers had to chuckle, and rebutted, "Come on Mary, give me what I need and I promise I'll take some Viagra."

Dinosa gave him Ramirez's address in San Jose, and added, "Good luck finding him. It seems he's dropped off the grid since the drive by."

"Thanks, Dinosa."

"You're welcome, Chalmers, and do me a favor. Save the Viagra."

***

Chapter Eleven

At 10:00 am the group met in the O'Farrell's den. Two new faces, but familiar to Chalmers, were in attendance.

"I'm sure you remember Mr. and Mrs. Steve and Nancy Cromwell," Ian said with a smirk.

Chalmers looked genuinely surprised and exclaimed, "I should have known."

In order to protect their anonymity as members of a Navy Seal team, those who participated in the mission to recover George Spinella, were known by their first names only. Not only did Chalmers not know their last names, he had no idea they were a married couple.

"It's great to see you two. I had no idea you were married," Chalmers said, shaking their hands and hugging them.

"Neither did the U.S. Navy while they were still our employer. Now that we're out it doesn't matter who knows," Nancy said.

"After talking with, or should I say being convinced by Ian, we decided our talents could be better served here," Steve said and added, "Jesse Leone is waiting for his early release request to be approved and should join us soon."

"It's great to have you," Chalmers beamed.

"Okay everybody, let's get this show on the road," Sean boomed, "Will you all find a chair, please."

He continued, "I think we should all be clear as to what our mission here is and I'd like to clarify and define what that is. First and foremost, we are gathered here to ensure that justice prevails for the slaughter and mutilation of the Barnes family and the attempted murder of John Garcia and his family. If our efforts disrupt and confuse the drug trade, so be it.

"We will pursue and bring to justice, Pablo Vasquez, the 'El Diablo' drug cartel and those who directly or indirectly participated in this crime as well as, from what Chuck Chalmers tells me, Hector Ramirez and his 'Mexican Mafia' gang, the ones responsible for the attempt murder of the Garcia's family.

"I'm happy to inform you we have recruited the best damned electronic information hacker in the world. We affectionately refer to him as 'Grub'. As we speak, he is sniffing into the finances of Pablo Vasquez and 'El Diablo'.

"We still haven't refined or finalized our plan, but we will keep you all briefed. In the mean time, I suggest you take advantage of the basement gym and the other amenities my home has to offer."

***

The gymnasium Sean had referred to would make the U.S. Olympic Committee proud. At one end of the huge room was a regulation sized half court basketball court. In the center of the room stood a boxing ring and at the other end in one corner was every piece of weight conditioning apparatus conceivable and the other corner was covered with a think tumbling mat. About fifteen feet above the floor a running track circled the room.

Ian handed Chalmers a boxer style head gear as they entered the gym from the adjoining shower and locker room.

"Here, put this on," Ian said and continued, "It's the only rule we have here."

Chalmers donned the head gear and observed Grant and Nancy engaged in some sort of hand to hand combat. Grant was approaching Nancy with a knife in his right hand. When he was about two strides from her, in the blink of an eye she stepped forward and grabbing the wrist holding the knife with both hands, she lifted his arm and ducking under it spun around. Grant fell to one knee and dropped the knife. She released one hand from his wrist and picked up the knife and with one swift movement made a simulated swipe that would have severed Grant's carotid artery.

It happened so fast Chalmers wasn't sure what he had just witnessed. Grant out weighed Nancy by a good one hundred pounds and here he was, sitting on the mat rubbing his wrist and forearm and smiling up at his foe.

"If you're obviously over powered, use stealth and speed," Ian chuckled.

Eyeing Chalmers up and down, Ian went on, "You look like you're in fairly good shape, considering."

"Considering what?" Chalmers interrupted, defensively.

"I'm just saying you should hit the weights and the track before we teach you in close battle tactics. Come on, do some stretching and then join me at the bench lift. I'll spot for you."

Ian was impressed with Chalmers' brute strength. Starting at one hundred pounds, Chalmers worked his way up to pressing two hundred and fifty pounds. A half hour later Chalmers found himself jogging at what he considered a fast pace, with Ian around the cat walk like track.

As they jogged, Chalmers asked, gasping, "How long are we going to do this?"

"Well, each lap is about two hundred yards. Ten laps is about one mile. I thought we'd just do ten laps this time," Ian replied.

"How many laps have we done?" Chalmers said, thinking his legs were about to burn off.

"Two and a half," Ian answered.

"Hey, Ian!" Colt yelled, standing on the gym floor looking up at them.

"Yeah?" Ian yelled, running in place as Chalmers was bent over trying to catch his breath and grateful for the respite.

"Your father would like to see you and Mr. Chalmers in his office ASAP."

"Thank you Jesus," Chalmers mumbled under his breath.

Colt handed them both towels and they followed him through the locker room and up the two flights of stairs. At the top, Chalmers stopped and said, "Hang on for a second, guys."

He picked up the plastic garbage can next to the stairwell door and proceeded to up chuck the wonderful oat bran muffins and orange juice Colleen had prepared for him that morning.

Wiping his face with the towel and replacing the garbage can, he said, "Okay we can leave now."

They entered Sean's office and Chalmers lost what little breath he had left.

"Jesus Christ, Dinosa! What are you doing here?"

She was sitting, dressed in full camo, in a leather chair in front of Sean's desk, giving Chalmers the evil eye.

"It seems Jeremy found Ms. Dinosa on the hill above the house apparently spying on us," Sean said.

"I am an officer of the law and I'm investigating a homicide. If you don't release me now, I will be forced to place…"

"For God's sake, Dinosa, did you follow me here?" Chalmers interrupted.

"Chuck, you've used me like I'm the camp whore and didn't even kiss me. I think I have the right to know what's going on here, even if I have a pretty good idea."

"And what is your idea of what's going on here?" Ian asked, suppressing a smile.

"I believe you've gathered together some people like that gorilla there," she said pointing to Colt, "to conduct some kind of operation to bring the filthy bastards that slaughtered the Barnes family to justice."

"Assuming you might be somewhat right, what do you propose to do?" Sean asked.

"I just started a four week vacation. Simply put, I'd like to join you."

Chalmers choked and said, "Mary, do you know what you're asking? Do you have any idea of what you'd be jeopardizing; you're career on the force, your reputation, your family's reputation, even time in prison if we're caught?"

"Don't any of you forget this; I was one of the first people to find this slaughtered family. It's an image that will go to my grave with me. And yes, Chuck, I know what I'm getting myself into. I'd strip naked in front of the Pope to be part of this team. In fact, I insist on it," Dinosa answered, her face flushed and a tear streaming from one eye.

The room fell silent. Sean looked at his son who nodded and then at Chalmers who just rolled his eyes.

"Well," Sean said, pushing his chair back and standing up, "bring your gym bag tomorrow and welcome aboard."

"Thank you Mr. O'Farrell. You won't regret it."

As the group left the room, Dinosa looked at Chalmers, his hair matted and his clothing wet from sweat.

"Jesus Chuck, you look like they've used you as the camp slut and you smell even worse," she said with a giggle.

***

The team spent the next week getting in shape and frequently meeting for strategy planning and briefings. At the end of the week, Sean gathered them in the den.

"Ladies and gentlemen," he started, "we're ready to kickoff operation 'Montezuma's Revenge'. We begin tomorrow morning with our first objective; the undoing of the 'Mexican Mafia.'

***

PART II

The Hunt

'First rule of the hunt; you eat what you kill.'
Quote from My Dad

Chapter Twelve

Dinosa picked up Chalmers in front of his house at 4:30 am the next morning.

"Did you remember your piece and cuffs?" she asked as he sat down in the passenger seat.

Chalmers gave her a, are you kidding me, look.

She repied, "Good," and handed him a badge holder with a gold shield.

"What's that for?" Chalmers said, pulling his sports jacket to reveal his belt with his shield attached.

"I didn't know they let you keep them after you retire."

"They do if you don't turn them in," he snapped.

"Jesus Chuck, why don't you untie that knot in your shorts?"

"Sorry Mary. It's just a little early for me."

They drove on in silence. Dinosa turned and drove up an on ramp and they continued south on the 280 Freeway. Forty minutes later they exited the freeway in San Jose, at Byrd Avenue and turned south. After several more turns they pulled up in front of a small white house on Little Orchard Drive. The sky over the East Bay Area hills was beginning to show the start of a new day.

Chalmers knew from a telephone conversation earlier in the week he had with Walter Jones, former member of the Bay Are Joint Task Force on Gang Activity and now Commander of the Alameda Sheriff's SWAT, that they were parked in front of home of Jose Maldonado. He had been informed that Maldonado was the president of Los Banditos, a motor cycle club associated with the 'Mexican Mafia' and responsible for distribution of the gang's drugs and smuggled arms.

Maldonado was also rumored to be one of the more ruthless enforcers of the gang. He was responsible for the murder of many rival gang members, including the bombing in Concord, California that wiped out an entire innocent family of five that lived next door to his intended target. He was never charged with causing this tragedy.

They approached the front door of the home with their guns drawn and held behind their backs. Chalmers banged on the front door, stepped back and waited. Dinosa, standing behind him kept her eyes on the front window. When the corner of the window shade was pulled back, revealing the head of a man, she yelled, "Go!"

Chalmers stepped forward and with a ferocious kick, knocked the door off its' hinges.

He bellowed, "Freeze, San Jose Police!" as he ran into the house, Dinosa right behind him.

The naked man took several steps and turned around with his hands raised.

"Hey man, this is police harassment," he whined.

Dinosa ran past the two men to a bedroom at the end of a short hallway. On the bed was a young woman sitting up holding the blankets to her breasts.

"Keep your hands where I can see them, Ma'am," she said with her gun pointed at the terrified woman.

In the front room Chalmers ordered the man to lie face down. He cuffed the man's hands behind his back He reached in his breast pocket and pulled out a photograph.

Holding the picture next to the man's head, he asked, "Are you Jose Maldonado?"

"I don't got to tell you shit," the man sneered.

"Thank you for being so cooperative, Mr. Maldonado," Chalmers said, as he pulled the man to his feet. "You're under arrest."

"Hey Tonto, bring this guy some trousers and a shirt," Chalmers yelled in to Dinosa.

A minute later she emerged from the hallway, the young woman in front of her was holding pants and a shirt. She looked at Maldonado as the woman struggled to put the pants on the cuffed man.

"What are you looking at, Punta," he sneered.

"Hmm, looks like a penis, only smaller," Dinosa quipped, looking at Chalmers.

As they walked Maldonado through the front, he turned his head and said in Spanish to the young woman, "Call 'Rapper' and tell him to get down to County and bail me out."

When they were outside, Chalmers pulled out a black hood that was stuffed in his belt and draped it over Maldonado's head.

"Hey man, you can't do that," he protested.

Chalmers bopped him on the back of his head with the butt of his pistol and said, "Shut up, I'm tired of you telling me what I can and what I cannot do."

"Oh man, my lawyer is gonna love this shit," Maldonado chuckled.

They stuffed him in the back seat of Dinosa's car and drove off. They travelled several blocks and made a right turn on Stauffer Street and a mile later turned right on the Monterey Highway and pulled into a warehouse parking lot. Ian and Grant were waiting at the front door.

Chalmers and Dinosa pulled Maldonado from the car and without saying anything, marched him past Ian and Grant and through the opened door. The two followed them in and Ian closed and locked the door. They proceeded across the abandoned reception area and down a hall with Maldonado in tow.

They stopped in front of a door and Chalmers removed the hood. Ian opened the door and ushered Maldonado into a six foot square room. He sat him down on a chair in the corner of the room behind a bolted down metal table and shackled his ankle to a leg of the table. He then removed the hand cuffs.

"What the fuck is going on. This ain't no fuckin' police station!" Maldonado protested, looking around the room.

Ian sat down on the chair across the table.

"Mr. Maldonado, I'm Detective Mickey Spade and I'll be conducting this interrogation," Ian said.

"I ain't answering shit. I know my rights and I want a lawyer, now!" Maldonado retorted.

"Before we get started, I know you've already been read your rights and signed the waiver, but I must remind you, you have the right to remain silent and if you cannot afford an attorney, one will be appointed for you."

"What the fuck are you talking about, that's what I just said, you stupid ben dejos."

"Okay, let's not pull any punches. We know you're a lieutenant in the 'Mexican Mafia' and you're Hector Ramirez's right hand man. We also know he ordered the hit on the Garcia family and the two of you slaughtered the Barnes family.

"You're facing the death penalty, pal."

"You ain't got shit man. I already told you I ain't given' you shit."

"We can promise you complete immunity if you cooperate. You're a little fish in the ocean, brother. We want your boss and his boss, Eric Morales. We want everything you know about the 'Mexican Mafia'."

"Dude, are you nuts or just stupid. I already told you I ain't saying shit and I want my lawyer!"

"I want you to know I appreciate your attitude and yes, we can place you and your family in witness protection," Ian said, anxiously leaning on his elbows across the table.

Maldonado looked bewildered. He put his hands to his face and mumbled in Spanish, "This is one stupid mother fucking cop." He removed his hands and looked at Ian and said, "Are you fucking crazy?"

"Good, good, now where can we find Hector Ramirez?"

"You gotta be fucking crazy."

The interrogation went on for another hour and then Ian said, "Jose, I'd like to thank you for your cooperation. Just hang tight and we'll have you out of here in no time."

Ian left the room and closed the door behind him. He met Grant in the hall, smiled and said, "Your turn."

Ian stuck his head in a room across the hall where Dinosa sat in front of a computer screen and said, "Okay, kill the video feed but make sure we capture the audio."

Grant slipped a black ski mask over his head. He entered the room bare from the waist up and glared down at Maldonado. His black muscular body loomed over the defenseless man. Failing to sound as tough as he wanted to, Maldonado looked up and said, "Who the fuck are you?"

"I'm your worst nightmare, and NOW you're going to answer my questions."

He reached down and picked up the much smaller man by his hair and slammed his fist into Maldonado's solar plexus, and in the same motion stepped to the side to avoid the spew of bile and stomach acid that jettisoned from the man's mouth.

Maldonado's eyes rolled up in his head as it twitched. Grant released his hair and he slumped down into his chair. Grant cuffed his hands behind him. He waited for the man to regain his senses and asked, "Are we ready to cooperate now?"

"Fuck you!" Maldonado said with even less machismo.

"Fine," Grant replied and pulled a switch blade from his back pocket.

With a loud click the razor sharp blade snapped out from the handle. Grant slipped it under the left cuff of Maldonado's jeans and ripped upwards. The baggy material tore easily under the pressure of the razor sharp edge.

When the blade reached the man's crotch, Grant paused and said, "Oh, did the big man pee pee himself, tsk, tsk?"

He continued with the knife until it reached a belt buckle loop. He repeated the maneuver on the other pant leg. He then slipped the knife under the tear just below the crotch and made a quick horizontal tear connecting it to the opposite leg. The blade nicked the man's scrotum on its' way.

Maldonado screamed in terror, "Okay, okay man. I'll tell you anything."

Grant calmly grabbed the two cut pieces of the pant legs and lifted them up, exposing the man's privates. He tied the two ends together behind Maldonado's neck. He snickered as he stepped back to admire his work.

Maldonado looked like he was wearing his pants as a bib, able to smell his own urine.

"I'm glad to see a change in your attitude. Now, where can we find Hector Ramirez?"

***

A half hour later Grant exited the room and walked across the hall and joined Chalmers, Ian and Dinosa. The three were gathered in front of a computer screen.

"Did you get enough?" Grant asked.

"I think so," Dinosa answered and continued, "The video's been streaming live to Grub."

Grub, known in the real world as Doctor Daniel Tanaka, was known as the 'hacker's hack' in the computer world. He was instrumental in recouping funds from George Spinella and redistributing them. He was from Hawaii and besides earning his doctorate degree in computer sciences, he had a list of credentials and published papers that would fill a bibliography page.

The screen blinked and was filled with Grub sitting at his desk.

"Hey guys, I got it all," he said.

"Hello, Grub," Ian said. "What else can we do?"

"Unless you can digitally manipulate and mix audio and video, there's nothing. Give me a couple of hours. Why don't you guys go grab some lunch?"

"Thanks, Grub, go do your thing," Ian said.

Grant drove down the street to a fast food drive thru and returned with burgers and cold drinks. He walked into the room that held Maldonado and sat a bag and drink on the table. Then he untied Maldonado's bib and removed the hand cuffs. Maldonado turned his head and cowered.

Grant said, "Enjoy," and left the room.

An hour and a half later, Grub was back on their computer screen.

He said, "Take a look at this and tell me what you think."

He clicked his mouse and suddenly the fuzzy image of the empty room across the hall appeared on their screen. The door opened and it showed Ian ushering Maldonado into the room. Ian shackled his ankle to the table and took off the hand cuffs and then sat down across from him.

From the camera's position and angle, the back of Maldonado's head could be seen as well as Ian sitting across from him.

Maldonado's head bobbed as he said, "What the fuck is going on? I already told you everything.'

"Mr. Maldonado, I'm Detective Mickey Spade and I'll be conducting this interrogation," Ian said.

The group continued to watch in amazement as they witnessed Ian ask the questions and Maldonado answering the same questions in the dialog he had with Grant. It was uncanny how realistic the dubbing was, down to Maldonado's head movement when he spoke the dubbed words.

When the video ended, Grub's face reappeared on the screen. "What do you think?" he asked.

"Grub, that was pure genius, amazing. Standby, we'll be contacting you in about an hour with the number where you can text that video and thank you," Ian said.

After shutting down and packing up the lap top, Ian turned to Chalmers and asked, "You've alerted your friend with Alameda County Sheriff SWAT and their standing by?"

"Commander Jones and his team are just waiting for an address," Chalmers replied

"Good, let's go turn Hector Ramirez's world up side down," Ian said with a smile.

They dressed Maldonado with a new pair of pants and escorted him to the loading dock area behind the warehouse where Grant was waiting in his car. They put Maldonado in the back seat and Ian got in the front passenger seat.

Chalmers and Dinosa stayed behind and cleaned up the scene, wiping down any evidence which could incriminate any of them and departed on the drive back to the O'Farrell estate in Sausalito.

Grant drove north on the 680 Freeway and exited at Milpitas and proceeded east into the hills overlooking Silicon Valley. He turned off of Skyline Boulevard into an upscale neighborhood on View Lane. They stopped several blocks into the neighborhood and pulled over to the curb.

Ian dialed Grub on his cell phone.

"Grub," he said, "do your mouse magic."

Grub lowered his voice and spoke eerily into the phone, "My work here is done. I must go now, elsewhere to where my super powers are needed."

Grant turned in the driver's seat and ordered Maldonado to turn his back to him in the rear seat. He uncuffed the bewildered man and ordered him to get out of the car.

"What the fuck is going on?" he asked.

"Would you rather go back to the warehouse?" Grant asked him.

Maldonado scrambled out of the car and Grant drove away and turned left at the next corner and double backed to Skyline Boulevard. He parked in a turn out across from View Drive. Ian got out of the car and walked across the street where he had a view looking down the hill on View Drive.

He watched as Maldonado appeared, walking up the hill looking around furtively. He approached a ranch style home and walked up the driveway.

Ian dialed the number Chalmers had given him earlier. He called Commander Jones and gave him an address on View Lane. He then walked back to the car and got in. He gave Grant the thumbs up sign and they drove off.

**

Jennifer sat in a recliner in the family room in front of the television. Suddenly she sat up and yelled, "Mom, Mom, come quick!"

Colleen rushed in from the kitchen just as the scene on the television switched to showing several people in hand cuffs being escorted from a ranch style home.

The news commentator was saying;

This was the scene shot earlier this afternoon at a home in the hills above Milpitas. Police say Alameda County Sheriff's SWAT raided the home after receiving an anonymous tip that alleged local leader of the 'Mexican Mafia', Hector Ramirez, wanted for questioning in a drive by shooting two weeks ago, by the San Francisco police, was hiding out there.

A police spokesman said the mutilated body of Jose Maldonado, a reputed lieutenant in the 'Mexican Mafia' street gang was discovered in a back bedroom of the home and Hector Ramirez, along with several other higher ups in his gang, have been taken into custody for the murder of Mr. Maldonado.

The spokesman also said ten kilos of cocaine and over one hundred pounds of marijuana was discovered and confiscated on the premises.

As we speak, it's reported that the Sheriff's Department have removed a section of backyard fence at the home and have off loaded a back hoe. This happening, the spokesman tells us, as a result of tips given by the same anonymous caller that they would find bodies buried there.

"Do you think Dad had anything to do with this?" Jennifer asked.

"I doubt it. Your father is away on a fishing trip."

"Yeah, I bet. Pop's never been fishing in his life," Jennifer said with a wry smile.

***

Chapter Thirteen

The traffic slowed as Chalmers and Dinosa neared the west end of the Richmond San Rafael Bridge. Dinosa lowered her driver's side visor to block the glare of the sun, setting over the coastal mountains.

"What do you think will happen to Maldonado?" she asked.

Chalmers was looking out the passenger side window, trying to avoid the glare.

"If he's lucky, they'll kill him fast," he said, and turning toward her he added, "It's probably not something we should dwell on."

"It's just that this is so fucking foreign to me. I mean, my whole life has been dedicated to upholding the law. I know I came into this with my eyes open, but how do you reconcile this?"

"Maybe I haven't, completely. You know, I asked Ian that same question during the Spinella recovery. He didn't really answer it except to say he felt better for doing it. We killed three people on that operation and his reasoning was, 'they all deserved it'.

"Maldonado committed a multitude of heinous crimes against the law and mother nature.

The law couldn't or wouldn't stop it. My respect for mother nature and the fact that I could is why I'm here."

Dinosa contemplated what her mentor had just said. She asked, "Why do you think law enforcement doesn't do more?"

"Wow, Mary, the answer to that question goes beyond my pay grade. I'm beginning to think Steve Cromwell has the right idea."

"And what does Cromwell think?"

"He believes we should change the laws. He believes we should surrender to win."

"What the hell does that mean?"

"The drug trade illegally generates tens of billions of dollars a year. That kind of money translates to power for evil people. It's the motivation for people like Pablo Vasquez to go to any means to obtain it. It's enough money to pay off greedy politicians and authorities to not only turn their heads but actually participate.

"The illegal drug business exploits everyone from the poor Columbian farmer who grows it to the miserable son of a bitch that will beg, borrow, steal or murder for it to feed his sick addiction," Chalmers said.

"So he would legalize it?"

"Yep, he says it's like liquor and prohibition. He compares the murder and violence created by illegal drug smuggling to the birth of organized crime during the liquor prohibition era. He believes if we legalized all of it we could control the price and generate tax revenue.

"If we eliminate the illegal distribution, we eliminate the crimes associated with it. Then we only have the demand side to deal with and he believes if we dedicated the resources, the money and manpower we now spend to eliminate the supply end, to educating and controlling the demand side, we're all better off, that simple."

They were nearing the end of the bridge and San Quentin Prison appeared to their south. Chalmers pointed at it and said, "See that prison? Over eight percent of its occupants are there for committing drug related crimes."

***

Chapter Fourteen

The group assembled in the O'Farrell den the next morning.

"Here's to a job well done," Sean said, lifting his cup of coffee.

He continued, "Thanks to the work we accomplished yesterday and the fine video that Grub produced, we have put a severe dent in the 'Mexican Mafia' and 'El Diablo's' ability to conduct business.

"Not only have Hector Ramirez and his group been indicted on murder charges and being held without bail, but my friend in the Alameda District Attorney's Office tells me the DA is presenting a strong case to Federal Prosecutors to indict Eric Morales, Ramirez and about ten others on Rico charges that include a host of criminal activity, including conspiracy to commit murder. He's sure that list will grow substantially.

"Grub is working on something he says will put the dagger in the 'Mexican Mafia's' heart.

"It's now time to go after the big prize, Pablo Vasquez and 'El Diablo'."

Ian stood up and walked to a white board. He picked up a black magic marker and said, "We believe phase one of operation 'Montezuma's Revenge', although not totally completed, has been successful enough to move on to phase two.

"We've divided up the group into two teams."

He turned around and writing on the white board, continued, "On Alpha team will be me, Chuck, Mary, Nancy and Steve. On Bravo team will be Grant, Jeremy and Jesse Leone, who's due to arrive this afternoon.

"Where do I fit in?" Garcia asked.

"John, you are the target of Pablo Vasquez and he has resources we don't even know about. You're too identifiable and high profiled to insert with the teams. Your presence could jeopardize the mission. You'll remain here with my father as operation coordinator and don't worry, we have something very special in mind for you.

"Timing and secrecy will be absolutely essential for the successful completion of this mission.

"Pack your sombreros and serapes; we're all going to Mexico. Our destination there will be Chapala.'

"The cover for Alpha team will be; you're a group of jet setters on holiday to party and play golf at several of the famous courses in the area. You'll be flying in our corporate jet to Guadalajara and renting a passenger van and driving to your rented hacienda at the Lomas del Chapala Country Club approximately six miles east of Chapala.

"Bravo team will travel as a bunch of fun loving guys going to Lake Chapala to enjoy their world famous bass fishing. You'll fly to Tucson, Arizona and pick up a large motor home with bass boat and trailer. From there you'll drive south to Chapala. Reservations have already been made for you at an RV park on the lake. Jesse knows the proprietor their.

"You've all been given a binder containing detailed maps and procedural strategies for each team, along with exit and subtraction plans. I suggest you review this information and we'll meet back here after breakfast tomorrow morning to go over it and get your input and answer questions."

As the group was breaking up, Sean grabbed Chalmers' arm and asked, "Chuck, could we have a word in my office?"

They entered his office and Sean said, "Chuck, I'm sure you've considered the danger surrounding this mission and the safety of your family. What are your plans?"

"Yes I have. I'm going to talk with Colleen this evening. I thought I would send them to my brother's place. He has a ranch in Colorado, and I think they will be safe there," Chalmers answered.

"Of course that's your decision, but if I could make a suggestion?"

"Sure, go ahead."

"I believe they would be safer staying here. You've probably seen some of the security we have installed and I can assure you we'll be beefing that up before the teams are deployed. You've met the other families staying here and I think Colleen and Jennifer would fit right in."

Chalmers thought about this for several moments and then said, "Thank you, Sean, for your generous offer. Let me think about it and talk it over with my family and I'll let you know later tonight."

***

That afternoon as Chalmers was driving home, he was thinking about how he would 'talk it over' with the family. Was he being selfish putting his family in peril? Would they understand? Should he just shelve this whole bloody mess and spend his time enjoying his family and being a good husband and father? He was confused and wrought with guilt as he pulled into the driveway next to his house.

He climbed the stairs and entered his home by the side entrance into the kitchen. No one was in the room, but he did notice three suitcases lined up next to the door. It piqued his curiosity.

"Hi, Babe," Colleen said, coming through the opening on the opposite side of the room.

"Wha...what's with the luggage? Are you going on a trip?" he stuttered with that confounded look that Colleen had come to love.

"You tell me," she said, walking to the refrigerator and pulling out two beers.

"Come on, let's go out on the deck and talk about it," she said.

When they were both comfortably seated under an umbrella table Colleen said, "You may not understand nor appreciated the fact that you don't just live with a couple of pretty faces."

Chalmers started to protest and was immediately interrupted.

"We know what you're up to and we know why you're doing it. After losing Jennifer's best friend and her family, we also know the dangerous nature of the people you're dealing with. After some long talks, understanding that you would protect us, we decided to defer to your judgment and go to wherever you thought best," Colleen said and then quickly added, "And don't fall all over yourself apologizing."

Chalmers sat gawking, open mouthed at her. He finally let out a big sigh of relief and said, "Geez, Honey, I should have known. Where's Jenny?"

"She went to the beach with friends. She should be gone long enough for us to get in a little 'hubbahubba'," she said, blushing sexually.

They moved to the bedroom and as Chalmers removed his shirt, Colleen said, "I don't think I can go through with this."

"Huh?" he said, confused.

"You've lost your love handles," she giggled

Later that evening, after supper, Chalmers called Sean to accept his offer.

***

Chapter Fifteen

"You know, Pop, you're gonna owe me and Mom big time," Jennifer said from the rear seat as they drove across the Golden Gate Bridge the next morning.

"Whatcha' mean?" Chalmers asked.

"I mean we were looking forward to going on a nice vacation for summer break," she replied.

"I'll tell what. When this is all over, I'll take you two wherever you want to go," Chalmers said.

"Any where in the world?" she asked excitingly.

Chalmers nodded, to which Jennifer exclaimed, "Mom, how about Tahiti or the French Riviera?"

Jennifer turned around and smiled at her daughter and said, "That'll give you something to think about."

A half an hour later they pulled up in front of the gate at the O'Farrell estate. It swung open and as they proceeded up the tree lined lane Colleen said, "Wow, this must be the way the other half lives."

Chalmers looked over at her smiling and said, "That was my thought exactly when I first saw this place."

Ian, his sister Sheila and her daughter Shannon, all stood at the bottom of the home's stairway to greet them.

After introductions were made, Sheila said, "Welcome to our home. Have you had breakfast yet?"

"Oh thank you very much, but we ate before we left our house this morning," Colleen replied.

"Well then, come in and we'll show you around and where you'll be staying," Sheila said.

The men grabbed the luggage from the trunk of the car and followed the women up the stairs and into the home. Once inside, Sheila led the group up stairs and escorted them down a hall to two bedrooms separated by a shared bathroom. The men sat the suitcases down and Ian turned to Chalmers.

"The others are already gathered in the den. We should join them," he said.

Shannon asked Jennifer if she liked to play basketball and when she told her she played on her girl's high school freshman team Shannon said, "Great, come on, we have a court in the basement," and they scampered off down the hall.

***

Sean started the meeting by having each team member explain the over all plan and his personal responsibilities. Questions were answered and suggestions made. Four hours later Ian summarized the briefing.

"We're dealing with a very sophisticated enemy that should not be underestimated. He has access to the same electronic equipment that we have. He may not be able to decode our communications, but he can certainly trace them.

"Once you're in Mexico, communication between teams should be held to a minimum.

We've established safe drop and pick up sites. Use them whenever possible.

"We'll meet here again after dinner tonight and discuss any last minute questions. Bravo team departs the day after tomorrow and operation 'Montezuma's Revenge' enters its next phase."

When the meeting broke up, Chalmers took his operation's manual out to the pool and sat down in the shade of the awning on the deck. Colleen was poolside, sun bathing with Sheila and chatting. Jennifer was taking turns diving off the three meter board with her new found friends. She seemed to be enjoying herself and he thought paying too much attention to Matthew O'Farrell.

Chalmers cracked the binder and began reading and studying the maps and drawings. It appeared that Ian and the rest of the group had planned every detail of the operation, including contingencies, but something still bothered him. What was it?

His biggest fear was that something would go wrong and he would be identified and Pablo Vasquez would seek revenge by harming his family. He had certainly demonstrated that he was capable of committing heinous crimes. He thought about the murder and mutilation of the Barnes family. Then it occurred to him. He stood up abruptly and walked back into the house.

He found Sean in his office with Ian.

"Yesterday you said you have something else in mind for John Garcia. What is it?"

"We probably should have briefed you earlier, but we decided it would be better to keep Bravo team focused on their mission as this phase will just be a little diversion before their deployment," Sean said.

He continued, "We think we've identified the 'El Diablo' mole inside the DEA."

***

PART III

The Hook

'You can't catch fish if you're hook's not in the water'
Another quote from my Dad

Chapter Sixteen

"Supervisor Luke Watson, please...I'd prefer not to say. Just tell him 'thunder and lighting'," Garcia said into the cell phone.

He and Sean were leaning on the pier rail overlooking Bodega Bay, about twenty miles north of San Francisco on the Pacific coast.

"John, is that you?" It was the voice of Luke Watson, an Operations Supervisor at the DEA in Arlington, Virginia.

"Yes Luke, it is," Garcia replied.

"Where the hell are you? We've been worried to death. You've got to come in!"

"Luke, I'm going to make this real quick and simple. My family and I are scared to death. We've been betrayed and I don't know who to trust except you. My family is safe and I won't tell even you where they are. If you want me to come in, I'll only surrender to you.

Be in San Francisco by noon tomorrow and I'll call you on your cell," Garcia said and hung up. He tossed the phone in the bay.

"Well, that should do it," Sean said and added, "Come on I'll treat you to lunch. 'Antonio's' over there serves the best steamed cracked crab in the Bay Area."

***

Sean and Garcia walked into the den back at the estate where the remainder of the group was gathered. It was 1:30 pm.

"Have we heard from our man in Arlington?" Sean asked.

"Yes and assuming your call was on schedule, he said Watson left the building about fifteen minutes after your conversation. He followed him for several blocks and into a park where Watson sat alone on a bench and made a phone call. Our guy was able to record what he said, but it's piss poor quality," Ian said.

"Let's hear it," Sean said.

Ian turned up the volume and hit the enter key.

Above the crackling could be heard, "Amigo, it's (something that sounded like high...doe). I just heard (indiscernible)... said he'd only surrender to me. (pause)...No I can't do that, it's too (indiscernible)...(pause)...Yes, okay (pause)...Tell them I'll call when I arrive. (pause...cackle)...Yes, yes, I understand."

"Our man says he then called his office and told them he was sick and wouldn't be back in today. He followed him to his car but lost him in traffic." Ian said.

"Let's get that recording to Grub and see if he can clean it up," Sean said.

"Already sent," Nancy said.

"Well, let's finish setting this up, then," Ian said.

***

Matt O'Farrell released the basketball from the top of the key and it clunked off the front of the rim.

"Ah ha, that's an 'e', I win!" Jennifer yelled.

Matt smiled and said, "You're not bad for a girl."

"What?!" Jennifer screamed, "I just kicked your ass in a game of horse and you say I'm okay for a girl?!"

She started to walk off toward the locker room.

"Ah, come on. I didn't mean it. Let's play to horses," he said, tossing her the ball.

She caught the ball and made a three point set shot.

"Ah shit, I give up. Let's go to the pool," he said, still smiling.

***

Garcia, Grant, Jesse, Steve and Nancy piled into the silver SUV parked in the driveway below the O'Farrell home. Ian was behind the wheel. The sun was just beginning to peek over the Berkeley hills across the bay.

They proceeded to drive down the tree lined lane and out to Alexander Avenue and up the hill to the 101 Freeway. Heading north on the freeway they took the Sir Francis Drake Boulevard west exit and traveled past the town of Mill Valley and into the foot hills occasionally passing clusters of homes. About two miles after they passed the Ignacio Valley Road and Sir Francis Drake Boulevard intersection, they turned left onto a gravel road. A half mile later the gravel road ended at a small abandoned cottage surrounded by oak trees. Ian pulled into the attached car port.

"Okay folks, we're home," Ian said as they exited the vehicle.

He retrieved a set of bolt cutters and a valise from the rear cargo area and walked onto the porch where he cut the lock securing the front door. They entered the home. It was sparsely furnished, but except for a layer of dust, appeared to be comfortable.

"Who owns this place," Nancy asked.

"I have no idea," Ian replied, and continued, "Let's get started. We know Watson will access satellite maps of the area when he finds out where John is, so he'll know the general topography.

"We also know he'll be meeting up with and will be in the company of at least two accomplices. He'll be instructed to come alone, so we think he'll drop off his people somewhere between here and the main road."

He reached into his valise and produced a satellite map of the surrounding area. He pointed to the house they were in and said, "I know we've been over this already, but lets review. This is where we are. Right here is a turn in the gravel road that can't be seen from the house. That's where we believe he'll drop off his accomplices.

"I want Steve and Nancy concealed in the trees here and here," he pointed to spots on the map on either side of the gravel road.

"By the time you're in position we should know how many people will be accompanying Watson and if they'll be in separate cars. At any rate, you will follow and observe any subjects dropped off. If things go south, you will eliminate them.

"Grant and Jesse, you will be positioned here and here," he continued, indicating points in the trees on either sides of the house. When the subjects approach the house, you will do your thing."

"Any questions?" he asked.

Receiving no replies he concluded, "Let's make the call. Who brought the thermos of coffee?"

***

"You know, this really chaffs my hide," Dinosa said.

She was sitting across the desk in Sean's office.

"What do you mean?" Sean asked.

"This fed, action Jackson, has 'f'ed up two of my homicide investigations and I'm about to hand him the biggest bust of his career," she said, shaking her head.

Sean was about to respond when the phone rang. He picked it up.

"Yes," he said, "That's great."

He hung up and looked at Dinosa, "You're up."

She reached in her handbag and brought out a cell phone and dialed. When she got through to Agent Jack Jackson, she said, "Yes, I have an anonymous tip about those murders in the Avenues and the drive by shooting in the upper Mission District that happened a couple of weeks ago."

"Ah...ah..., Inspector Dinosa?" Jackson stuttered.

"I said I was an anonymous caller. Do you want the tip or not?"

"Oh...yes, of course," he said.

"If you and your team are at the corner of Sir Francis Drake Drive and Ignacio Valley Road, it's west of Mill Valley, at noon today and you give me your cell number, I'll call you and let you know where you can catch some big fish," Dinosa said, trying hard to keep a straight face.

Jackson told her his cell phone number and Dinosa said, "By the way agent Jackson, when you guys get there, you should stay out of sight, and don't fuck it up."

Dinosa hung up the phone and removed its' battery.

Sean looked at his watch and said, "Well, we can only wait now. What do you say we do it out by the pool?"

***

Chalmers stood behind the crowd waiting to greet passengers at the bottom of the stairs and escalator in the south building at San Francisco International Air Port. He recognized Watson as he descended on the crowded escalator.

After they had listened to the cleaned up version of the audio tape Grub had made the night before, they now knew what had sounded like 'high doe' was really 'Hidalgo' and was Watson's code name to 'El Diablo'.

Chalmers looked at this watch. It read 10:35 am. He dialed his cell phone and said, "Hidalgo has arrived."

He knew Watson had reserved a Hertz rentacar and he hurried to the Hertz kiosk and waited. After Watson picked up the keys to his car he followed him outside and onto the Hertz shuttle bus. As the bus entered the rental car parking lot he noticed Jeremy Colt parked in the 'customer pickup' area.

He followed Watson at a safe distance through the parking lot until Watson spotted his rental car and started towards it. Chalmers picked up his pace and as Watson depressed the unlock button on his key chain at the rear of the car, he approached him and said, "Jesus, I hate this. I'm looking for aisle 'G'. Do you have any idea where that might be?"

Watson turned around annoyed and pointing up to a sign attached to a light standard said, "Since this is aisle 'D', I would guess it's three aisles down."

"Oh, thanks," Chalmers said, and when Watson turned around he attached a tracking device on the inside of the rear wheel well.

Chalmers walked around the parking lot appearing to be lost until Watson had pulled out and was driving toward the parking lot exit. He hustled back to the awaiting Jeremy and jumped into the car.

He picked up a palm pilot off the dash. The screen showed a map of the area and a red blinking light indicated where

Watson's rental car was. They followed it out of the air port exit and north onto the 101 Freeway. It exited on the Third Street exit and they followed it. Chalmers realized they passed within a few blocks of the converted warehouse loft where Dinosa lived. They now had a visual of Watson's car a block and a half ahead.

Watson pulled over into a bus loading zone and stopped. Colt drove past him and noticed in his rear view mirror two Hispanic looking men get into Watson's car. Chalmers watched as the blinking dot doubled back and got back on the 101 freeway going north.

They followed it through the city and onto the Golden Gate Bridge. When it exited at St. Francis Boulevard, Chalmers made a phone call. He simply said, "Hidalgo ETA fifteen minutes."

He looked at his watch which read 11:50 am. "Just like clock work," he said to Colt, and added, "Let's go home."

Watson turned onto the gravel road. Just as predicted, he dropped his two passengers off just out of view from the cottage. The two men pulled semiautomatic pistols from under their shirts and crept to either side of the road and walked forward. They stopped when the cottage came into view.

Watson pulled up behind the SUV and got out of his car. He walked to the front door and knocked.

"Come in," Garcia said, sitting in an easy chair pointed toward the door.

Watson entered and Garcia said, "So good to see you, Hidalgo."

"What the…" Watson stammered.

"Keep your hands where I can see them," Ian said, stepping out from the kitchen with his forty caliber pistol pointed at Watson's head.

Garcia picked up a machete that lay next to the easy chair and stood up. He put the razor sharp edge up to Watson's neck and said, "Now, you're going to do exactly what we say, or I swear to God, you'll look like the crime scene photos of the Barnes' family with your head propped between your legs when they find you."

Less than five minutes later Watson opened the front door and walked several steps out onto the porch. He yelled out, "Miguel, Pedro, it's all clear! Come on up!"

The two men emerged from the tree line and headed toward Watson, their weapons still drawn. When they were about thirty feet from him two loud, almost simultaneous pops were heard. Both men grabbed their necks. Pedro fell immediately to the ground motionless. Miguel stumbled forward two steps, his eyes rolled back in his head and he dropped to the ground. The tranquilizer darts had found their marks.

Grant and Jesse came out from behind their concealed spots and Steve and Nancy walked up the gravel road. They picked up the unconscious bodies and carried them inside the tree line behind the cottage.

Ten minutes later the SUV carrying the team passed the intersection at St. Francis Boulevard and Ignacio Valley road. The only sign of human activity Ian saw was a man pacing back and forth behind some shrubs.

Ian smiled and dialed his cell phone, "Hidalgo and posse secured, you can send in the cavalry."

On the other end Dinosa grinned and gave the thumbs up to Sean, who was sitting next to her by the pool.

She hung up and immediately dialed Agent Jackson and told him where he could find the fish. Unable to help herself, she added, "You may want to give channel six a heads up so you can get some face time on the five o'clock news. And remember, the next time you want to fuck this anonymous caller, have the decency to kiss her first."

***

Everyone was gathered in the O'Farrell den sprawled out in front of the big screen television. The five o'clock news was on. The anchor was saying;

A fortuitous anonymous tip led FBI agents to a cottage outside the town of Mill Valley this afternoon that may lead to solving the mystery surrounding the slayings of the Barnes family and the drive by shooting at a DEA agent's home, both occurring in San Francisco a little more than two weeks ago.

We now go live to the Federal Building in downtown San Francisco for live coverage of the press conference called by FBI Special Agent Jack Jackson.

The scene shifted to Jackson standing behind at least have a dozen microphones and in front of a group of journalists.

I'm proud to announce, as the result of some excellent investigative work by local law enforcement and the FBI, and with the help of a good Samaritan anonymous citizen, we have today arrested Luke Watson, an Operations Supervisor with the DEA whom we believe was an informant for the 'El Dorado' drug cartel and was instrumental and an accomplice to the recent slaying of the Barnes family and driveby shooting of a DEA agent here in the city. The mutilated bodies of two Mexican Nationals, identified as Miguel Blanco and Pedro Rodriguez, believed to be the actual perpetrators in the Barnes family slaying, were found near the location where Mr. Watson was arrested.

Preliminary DNA testing indicates both Blanco and Rodriguez were present at the time of the Barnes family murders. The investigation of DEA operative Watson's involvement is ongoing.

"That man's timing is impeccable," Dinosa said.

Chapter Seventeen

The thirtysix foot Itasca motor home easily negotiated the steep winding two lane road up into the Mezquita Mountains about thirty miles south of Durango, Mexico. It was 11:00 pm, local time. Jesse Leone was behind the wheel, Jeremy Cold sat next to him in the passenger seat and Grant Wilson was asleep in the bedroom at the rear of the motor home. They had not seen nor passed another vehicle since they passed through Durango about fortyfive minutes ago.

As the RV made a sharp turn, they saw a sixties model Cadillac parked in a turn out. When they passed, the Cadillac's headlights came on and it pulled out behind them.

"I counted two heads. This doesn't look good," Colt said, turning around. "Grant, look alive!" he yelled.

The next turn was a blind curve and as they came out of it they saw a Humvee parked across both lanes about one hundred feet ahead blocking the road. Jesse applied the brakes and stopped about twenty feet from where a man in uniform stood in front of the Humvee. Two more men, dressed in shabby looking uniforms stood behind him with AR16s slung over their shoulders. The Cadillac pulled up behind them and two men got out, also carrying AR16s.

The leader approached the driver side window, unholstering his revolver. The two men from the Cadillac stood on either side of the boat and trailer behind the RV.

"I got this one. Grant, are you okay," Jesse said.

"I gottem'," Grant replied, looking out a window slat in the rear of the RV.

"You take the other two," he said to Colt, and added, "On the count of three."

He slid the driver's side window open and said, "Buenos notches, amigo."

The man replied in broken English, "Everybody get out of the vehicle with your hands up."

"Uno momento, por favor," Jesse said, bending down.

"One, two, three," he said, sitting back up with his 9mm. In one swift move, he aimed and shot the uniformed man between his eyes.

At the same time, Colt leapt from the passenger side door and shot the two others before they could unshoulder their weapons. In the rear of the RV, Grant first shot the man to his right and then the one on his left, who stumbled off the shoulder of the road and screamed as he tumbled down an almost shear cliff.

"Let's clean up this mess," Grant said, disgustedly.

They put the dead bodies in their vehicles and pushed them off the road into the steep ravine. The sound of scraping metal and loud bangs was all that could be heard as the cars disappeared into the dark.

"Jesus, what if we were just a family on vacation?" Grant asked, as they got back into the RV.

"We'd probably never be seen or heard from again," Jesse said.

Colt added, "Just last week, an elderly couple from Minnesota was driving their motor home to Mazatlan and never showed up. It's something the Mexican chamber of commerce doesn't like publicized and neither does our State Department."

"We've got at least six hours before the sun rises and these guys are discovered. We should be at Lake Chapala by then," Jesse said.

The sun was peaking over the lake's horizon when they pulled off the Gonzalez Gallo Highway and drove down a gravel road that lead to Lake Chapala's northwest shore. They parked in front of a large adobe home and got out of the RV.

They were all stretching and working out the kinks when they heard a door slam.

"Semper fi, ya little fucker," a smallish, lean and well weathered man who looked to be closing in on sixty, cried, approaching the group from the adobe home.

"Sergeant Sam, you old bastard, you haven't changed a bit," Jesse said, shaking the man's hand and then hugging him.

Sam Francis was Jesse's platoon sergeant and drill instructor in Marine boot camp thirteen years ago. Sam had followed Jesse's military career through Navy Seal training and several years thereafter before he retired. They had since maintained contact.

He was married to Maria, a Mexican National, and after he retired from the Marine Corp they bought this home and RV park and moved their family of eight children to Lake Chapala eight years ago.

After introductions were made, Sam said, "I put you in that first space past the house. When you get settled, come on back to the house and meet the family."

***

The wheels of the Cessna Citation sat down on the runway of Guadalajara International Airport. The plane taxied to the designated area for international flights where several customs' officials met the passengers as they debarked.

After a baggage cart was loaded with golf bags and luggage, the team was led across the tarmac and into a building. Pass ports were checked and stamped and a per functionary inspection of their luggage was performed.

Once outside, the team loaded the rear of a waiting van with the golf bags and luggage.

The rental car attendant handed Ian the keys to the van and the team piled in. Chalmers took the front passenger seat and Dinosa, Steve and Mary crawled into the back. They headed south on Highway Twentythree for the hour trip to Lomas del Chapala Country Club.

As they crested the hill, a lush green valley appeared before them and beyond that the blue waters of Lake Chapala. The view took Dinosa's breath away and she gasped, "In the middle of Mexico, who would have thought?"

They passed through the town of Chapala and turned east on the Gonzalez Gallo Highway. They drove by lush coffee plantations and vineyards and six miles later they turned left on Los Lomas Drive, which bypassed the club house and restaurant and skirted the perimeter of the golf course. A half mile later they made a left onto Los Lomas Court. At the end of the court sat 'Hacienda Grande', their home for the next week or so.

They parked in the circular driveway below the home and unloaded. As they trudged up the stairs to the front entrance of the house, carrying luggage and golf bags, Steve said, "Some digs. Do you O'Farrell's know anything but first class?"

The home sat on three levels. The front door opened onto the lowest level and a large foyer area with a windowed wall on the far side that led to a large wide deck that ran the length of the house and overlooked the third tee box on the golf course. To the right of the entrance area, stairs led to the next level where there was a living room and dining room connected to an open kitchen. On the third level were four bedrooms, each with a private bathroom and outside lanai.

"After everyone's unpacked, let's meet on the deck and go over our next move," Ian said as they ascended the stairs to the third level.

***

Chapter Eighteen

"Well, both teams arrived safely at their destinations and are in place," Sean said as he took a chair next to Garcia in the shade on the poolside deck.

"Yeah, and it's driving me nuts. I've always been a field man. Being this, what did you call it, 'Operation Coordinator', sucks."

"I knew you'd understand," Sean chuckled.

"You know what I don't understand? Let's say this operation is successful. What will it accomplish? Sure, we will have avenged the Barnes family. We will have destroyed a drug cartel, but you know what? Somebody will take Vasquez's place."

"We've taken down a corrupt DEA official," Sean said tentatively.

"Yeah, we've done that, but with the billions of dollars up for grabs in the graft pot, who knows how high up the corruption goes? I know it goes higher than one junior official at the DEA.

"Will our effort make a difference for the poor dirt farmer who grows the leaves to the poor bastards that are addicted to it and all the innocent victims in between? Let's face it, I know the focus of our efforts is to bring to justice the people who savagely slaughtered the Barnes family, but in the end, will it make the world any safer for them?" Garcia said, pointing at his children and the other young people playing water volleyball.

"John, we can only fight one battle at a time," Sean replied.

"I know, that's why when this is done, I'm going to ask for your help, again," Garcia said.

***

Chapter Nineteen

The three 'fishermen' were ushered into Sam's house by his thirteen year old daughter, Angela. In the far corner of the room was a large open kitchen and beyond that was a screened in dining room.

Sitting at the elongated table with his wife and three other children, Sam said, pointing at a counter adjacent to the kitchen, "Hey fellas, come on in. Grab a cup of coffee and a plate and have a seat."

Sam introduced his family and then said, "Help yourself."

A large pan of tortilla de huevos sat in the middle of the table next to a tin of cornbread muffins. The men dished up large portions and sat down.

After polishing off their plates the men each thanked Sam's wife, Maria. The four children aged twelve to seventeen, sat staring wide eyed at the three strangers.

"Hey kids, it's chore time," Sam said.

The children got up and reluctantly left the room. Maria began clearing the table.

"What can you tell us about Pablo Vasquez?" Jesse asked when the four men were alone.

"I can tell you he's a cock sucker," Sam began.

"He's the dictator in these parts. He owns this part of the world and if you get in his way, he simply eliminates you. His parents were poor, hard working dirt farmers from the mountains just north of here. I guess he didn't care for that life.

"He moved here shortly after we did about ten years ago. At the time Chapala was a sleepy little tourist village, catering to mostly Yankee fisherman. He bought or stole most of the real estate around here, plus most of the businesses in town. He's left us pretty much alone, probably because there's not enough profit in a RV park.

"When he first arrived he faced some resistance, but quickly dispensed of those who would stand up against him. The local police chief and his family were found decapitated in their home. Any business or land owner who wouldn't sell out to him came to the same fate. I understand now he has every State official in his pocket.

"You're taking on one ruthless hombre, and make no mistake, I'll do what I can, but I won't put my family in jeopardy. They have suffered enough already."

"We understand and we appreciate what you've already done. Do you know any of his daily routine? What he likes, where he goes, things like that? We know he's a golf enthusiast, anything else?" Jesse asked.

"Yes, he loves his golf. My oldest son is a bartender in the lounge at Lomas del Chapala golf course and he tells me Vasquez has a regular tee time at three pm on Tuesdays and Thursdays. He also plays regularly at the Chapala Country Club which is about three miles west of Chapala.

"My oldest daughter works as a receptionist at Hotel del Chapala. Cabaret del Chapala, is the night hot spot here and is attached to the hotel. Both, by the way, are owned by Senor Vasquez. Juanita, my daughter says he usually frequents the cabaret on Friday and Saturday nights.

"He's never been seen alone. He travels in a black limousine with two bodyguards and is followed by a black SUV with at least two more thugs inside."

"Do you know who he plays golf with and if any of his thugs accompany him on the course?" Jesse asked.

"No, but I can find out," Sam answered.

"Sam, I hope you know we don't want to put you or your family in any danger. I'm just an old Marine buddy visiting you with some good old boys on a fishing trip," Jesse said.

"Believe me Jesse, I wouldn't have agreed to help you if I knew any different," Sam said.

Jesse stood up and shaking Sam's hand, said, "Well guys, let's go fishing."

***

"What do you think?" Nancy said, holding up a brightly colored blouse to her chest.

Dinosa looked over from where she was thumbing through a circular rack of skirts and replied, "It's perfect. Buy it."

They were inside a small clothing boutique that bordered the town square. The two were on what Nancy had earlier told her husband, "The mother of all shopping sprees."

She paid for the blouse and they continued their stroll, laded with bags and boxes, through the plaza. They came to a sidewalk bar called 'Cisco's' and Dinosa said, "All this shopping has made me thirsty. What do you say?"

"Let's do it," Nancy answered.

They both put down their packages and pulled a stool out and sat down. Dinosa placed her shoulder bag on the bar and they both ordered pina coladas. When the bartender delivered their drinks she noticed him slip an envelope into her bag.

They sipped their drinks and talked nonsense. After finishing their drinks, they gathered their cargo and walked across the plaza where a line of taxi cabs were queued in front of the Hotel del Chapala. They got in the first one and rode back to 'Hacienda Grande'.

The men were sitting on the deck drinking beer when the women entered the front door. They dropped their packages and went out to join them. Dinosa handed Ian the envelope. He opened it and withdrew the note. It was from Jesse.

After reading it he passed it to Chalmers and said, "Looks like we'll be doing some clubbing."

Chalmers finished reading the note and passing it to Steve, said, "It's Thursday, isn't it?"

And looking at his watch added, "And it's three fifteen. What do you say we meet Senor Vasquez?"

The three men grabbed their beer bottles and walked over and leaned against the deck railing above the third tee. They didn't wait long when three carts rounded some oak trees and came into view. The first cart was driven by Pablo Vasquez. Another man sat beside him. The second cart had two fellow players and in the last cart were two large Hispanic men dressed in white cotton trousers and shirts with Uzi automatic pistols in their laps.

The carts pulled up behind the tee box and the golfers got out. The two men in white stayed in their cart and looked around. One of them noticed the three men standing above them on the deck and pointing at them said something to his partner.

Chalmers raised his glass and yelled down, "Salut!"

That got the group's attention and they all looked up. Several tipped their hats in return and Chalmers tipped his bottle.

Vasquez was first on the tee box and hit a good shot down the middle of the fairway.

Ian yelled out, "Go in the hole!"

Vasquez turned and looked up at him, obviously annoyed. He retrieved his tee and walked over to the cart with the two bodyguards in it and said, "Who are the fucking gringos in the 'Grande Hacienda'?"

When both men shrugged Vasquez said, "Find out."

The smaller of the two men pulled a cell phone from his breast pocket and dialed. After a brief conversation he walked over to Vasquez and said, "The club's Visitor Accommodator says the man's name who reserved the house is Fred McAllister. He's the Chief Financial Officer for a U.S. company called 'S and G Imports'. He's here with his son and daughterinlaw and another married couple."

"Did you say 'S and G Imports'?" Vasquez asked rhetorically.

***

Jesse pulled off the dirt road into a corn field and parked Sam's borrowed pickup truck just out of view from the road. He, Steve and Grant got out of the truck and crossed the road and disappeared into a forest of banyan trees and thick under brush.

The half moon night provided sufficient light to illuminate the surrounding geography as if it were daylight, seen through the night vision glasses they all wore. The landscape began to descend at a slight angle and the men slowed their pace.

They emerged from the forest and found themselves atop an almost sheer rock cliff. Three hundred feet below them lay the Vasquez estate.

Steve pulled a night vision camera fitted with a telephoto lens from his backpack and began taking pictures while Jesse and Grant busied themselves installing pitons in the granite rock which would accommodate rappelling ropes for their eventual descent to the valley below. They stashed their back packs in the nearby bushes and hustled back to the truck and drove to the RV park.

Once inside the Itasca, Steve connected his camera to a lap top and began down loading the pictures he had just taken. Grant rolled out a map on the table next to the lap top that showed satellite images of the Vasquez estate.

"Well, we confirmed a frontal assault is out of the question," Jesse said, pointing to the fortified gate that guarded the main entrance. An eight foot adobe fence extended on either side of the gate and surrounded the five acre grounds. Spaced approximately every one hundred feet a small device could be seen mounted on top of the wall. The team had identified them as closed circuit video cameras, probably armed to start by motion detectors.

Beyond the gate was a road that led to the main highway and passed a large warehouse that doubled as an air plane hangar. Stretching out from the hangar was a quarter mile long runway.

They scrolled through the photographs Steve had taken. Two armed men guarded the gate. At least four others patrolled the inside perimeter, two of whom were accompanied by German Sheppard's. The home was well lighted that provided few blind spots or shadows. Two men could be seen guarding the front entrance to the house and two more at either end of the home.

A watchtower sat in the far corner behind the house, occupied by one person who stood behind a swivel mounted machine gun. To his right was a large spot light. The tower was high enough to allow its' occupant a view of the entire grounds.

"This is one paranoid son of a bitch," Grant whistled.

Jesse pointed at the watchtower in the photograph and said, "That will be target number one."

***

"Holy shit," Dinosa groaned, attempting to wave away the smoky fog that filled 'Cabaret del Chapala'.

A Mexican band blared music from a stage on the opposite side of the room as the group entered. In front of the stage was a dance floor now crowded with people dancing to the reggae tune. Surrounding the dance floor were tables for four and booths lined the walls.

A young lady in a full length low cut gown approached the group and escorted them to a three sided booth. As they made their way across the room, Chalmers noticed Pablo Vasquez sitting in a large corner booth at the opposite side of the room. Vasquez was flanked on one side by a pretty blond girl and on the other by a beautiful young Hispanic girl. On either side of them sat two large, shaved headed Hispanic men and on the end sat a smaller man engaged in conversation with Vasquez.

As the group settled into their booth, Dinosa and Nancy ordered Singapore Slings and the men ordered Corona beers. Before their drinks arrived, Dinosa elbowed Ian and said, "Come on, let's dance."

Ian reluctantly followed her out onto the dance floor when the drinks arrived. As the hostess delivered the drinks, she bent over, revealing a healthy cleavage, and said to Chalmers in broken English, "These are compliments of Senor Vasquez," and pointing to Vasquez she added, "He has requested you visit him, if it's no problemo."

"It's no problemo," Chalmers said.

He stood up with beer in hand and started across the room. Vasquez said something to the little man who rose and left as Chalmers arrived at the table.

"Mister McMillan, so nice of you to accept my invitation, please have a seat," Vasquez said, smiling friendly.

"Senor Vasquez, have we met?" Chalmers asked curiously.

"No, I don't think so, but it has come to my attention that you are the CFO of 'S and G Imports' in the States. You may have heard of one of my companies, 'Los Exportar'."

"Hmm, I seem to remember we did business with 'Los Exportar' several years ago, but I was just the Accounting Department Manager then and I have no direct knowledge," Chalmers replied.

"I was hoping we could discuss renewing our business association," Vasquez said.

"Senor Vasquez, I would be happy to entertain any proposal you may have, but right now I'm on holiday with my son and daughterinlaw and their friends, and I rarely mix business with pleasure."

Vasquez reached in his inside jacket pocket and withdrew an envelope. Handing it across the table to Chalmers, he said, "I can appreciate that. Perhaps you and your friends can join us for dinner tomorrow night and we can discuss my proposal then. I'm sure it could prove to be a very personally profitable opportunity."

Chalmers peeked in the envelope and saw a one inch stack of one hundred dollar bills. He looked up, smiled and said, "That's very generous of you and I'm sure we would love to accept your invitation."

"Good, very good, I'll have my car pick you up at the 'Hacienda Grande' tomorrow night, say around eight," Vasquez said.

"If you don't mind, I must insist on driving our vehicle. I hate going to strange places without my own car. If you could just give me directions to your home, I can get us there. I hope you understand," Chalmers said, trying to sound appreciative.

Vasquez thought for a moment and said, "Of course, I feel the same way."

He jotted down his address and directions on a napkin and handed it to Chalmers.

"Senor Vasquez, I appreciate your hospitality, but I really should be getting back to my party. I look forward to dinner tomorrow night," Chalmers said, standing and extending his hand.

Shaking Chalmers' hand, Vasquez said, "Good to meet you and I hope this is the beginning of a long friendship. By the way, your tab for tonight is taken care of, enjoy."

Chalmers returned to his table. As he passed the dance floor he caught Nancy's eye and winked. She threw a sexy hip in his direction and spun around, grabbing Steve's hand.

***

Nancy and Dinosa sat their packages down and pulled up a stool at 'Cisco's'. Garcia and Jeremy stood across the plaza haggling prices with a street vendor pedaling leather goods.

They covertly watched as the two women ordered drinks and exchanged envelopes with the bartender.

The two women finished their drinks, got up and strolled laughing and chatting toward the taxi stand. Jeremy pulled a wad of bills from his pocket and bought two leather shoulder bags from the street vendor. They walked across the plaza to 'Cisco's and ordered two beers and received the envelope left by the women.

Nancy and Dinosa got in the back seat of the cab and gave the driver directions to 'Hacienda Grande'. They drove to the edge of town when the driver said in broken English, "Please, I give my cousin a ride."

Before they could protest, the cab pulled to the side of the road and a young man dressed in sandals, cutoff jeans and a stained tee shirt jumped in the passenger seat. He turned and pointed a pistol at the two surprised women in the back seat.

"No problemo senoritas, we jus gonna rob you," the driver said, and turning to his friend, said in Spanish, "We're going to have fun with these two."

Nancy turned to Dinosa and, feigning terror, said, "Olowfay ymay eadlay," and then turning back to the men looking dumbfounded at each other, she said, "Oh please, please don't hurt us."

Dinosa cried, "We have money. We can pay you."

"Oh yeah, this is going to be a lot of fun," the man holding the pistol cackled.

The taxi turned off the main highway onto a dirt road that led them past a vineyard and into a grove of trees. They parked and the two women were ordered out of the car and led into the trees.

The man holding the gun said, "Alto, now take off you clothes."

Nancy turned around facing the man with the gun and reaching down with both hands pulled her tee shirt out of her jeans and lifted up. When it was over her head she stepped forward and yanked it off and wrapped it around the man's gun hand and pulled hard. She spun and threw her body into the man and drove her knee into the side of his knee. The man screamed and crumpled to the ground dropping the pistol.

Almost simultaneously, Dinosa, wearing light hiking boots, kicked the other man in the crotch, the hard toed boot catching him squarely in his testicles. He let out a whoof, grabbed his crotch with both hands and fell to his knees, looking mercifully up at Dinosa.

Nancy retrieved the pistol and pointing it at the cab driver said in perfect Spanish, "Who's having fun now?" and spit on him.

She ordered both men to undress and when they were reluctant to do so she put the barrel of the gun to the driver's forehead and cocked the revolver. "I said now!"

The driver had to help the man with the broken knee out of his cut offs. When the driver dropped his trousers, his scrotum was already beginning to swell and turning an ugly blue.

Dinosa looked at his penis and said with a sneer, "You were gonna have fun with that?" and spit on him.

Nancy slipped her shirt back on and noticed it was stretched and a little wrinkled. She looked at Dinosa and said, "What do you think?"

Dinosa replied with a wide grin, "It's perfect, let's go."

They collected the men's clothes and holding them with outstretched arms deposited them in the trunk of the cab. Nancy drove and as they pulled away from the two pathetic men sitting naked under a banyan tree, she said, "Well, enough fun for one day, we really should be getting home." They both nervously laughed hysterically.

***

When Grant and Jeremy arrived back at the RV park they found Jesse and Sam shooting the breeze on the front porch of Sam's house. They took a chair on the porch and Maria soon arrived with two cold beers for them and disappeared back into the house.

"Did they pick up the pictures?" Jesse asked.

Grant nodded and withdrew an envelope from his rear pocket and handed it to Jesse. He unopened the envelope and read the note's content.

Standing up, Jesse said, "Ian wants a face to face," and glancing at his watch added, "He'll be here in fifteen minutes and it looks like tonight is DDay. We should get back to the RV."

Ten minutes later there was a knock on the RV's door and Ian entered. The satellite map and the photographs were sprawled out on the table. They reviewed the material and then Ian said, "I assume you've developed a plan to take out the outside security."

He looked at Jesse who said, "Yes we have. The biggest challenge will be timing. We have to make sure our attacks start simultaneously. As soon as we take out the tower guard, we're committed. You'll have to identify the command center inside and take out the man watching the monitors first."

"We'll handle the inside security. You'll be at the back of the house. Keep an eye on the rear windows. When you see a room light flash twice, it's a go. If it flashes four times, it means the mission is aborted and get the hell out of there," Ian said.

He continued, "We're supposed to arrive at eight tonight and we'll delay that and plan on arriving about eightfifteen. It should be dark enough by then for you to rappel the cliff undetected. After we arrive, we'll give you at least half an hour to get in position. Following that the signal could come at anytime. Any questions?"

When no one responded, he said, "Good hunting," and departed.

***

PART IV

The Hit

"Keep a clear eye, and hit 'em where they ain't,"
Quote by 'Wee' Willie Keeler, who played baseball for the
Baltimore Orioles at the turn of the twentieth century, in response
to the question, what is your secret to being such a great hitter?

Chapter Twenty

Sam stopped his pickup truck along the corn field next to where Jesse had parked it the night before. Jesse, Grant and Jeremy exited the truck and grabbed their back packs from the truck's bed.

Jess walked around to the driver's side and through the open window said, "Hey compadre, thanks for everything. We'll see you later."

Sam reached around Jesse's head, pulled it close and whispered in his ear, "Good hunting my friend."

The three men, wearing black and dark green camos with face makeup to match and black dorags covering their heads, made their way to the edge of the cliff. They retrieved the gear they had stashed the night before and attached one end of coiled rope to the pitons.

Jesse looked at his watch. It read 8:05 pm. The sun had set and the valley below was dark. A bit of twilight was cast across the western skyline. The men cast their coils of rope off the cliff and retrieved enough to attach their repelling harnesses. Squatting, they peered down the valley and waited.

Five minutes later they saw headlights coming down the road. The lights stopped at the gate and a minute later proceeded toward the home. The three men gave each other the thumbs up sign and bailed off over the cliff's rim.

***

Ian noticed two men at the front door of the home and two more at either end of house as he maneuvered the van and parked it behind a black SUV at the entrance walkway. One of the two men standing at the door came down to greet them.

He was wearing a shoulder holster housing a semiautomatic pistol.

As they neared the archway entry to the home the door opened and Pablo Vasquez stepped out.

"Buenos noches, my friends and welcome to 'El Diablo Hacienda', he said jovially.

He shook Chalmers hand and was introduced to the rest of the group. They entered the foyer and entrance area of the home. A large crystal chandelier hung from the high ceiling in the center of the room and a wide stairway that tapered as it reached the upstairs rose to their right. Ian noticed a room to the left in the front corner of the entrance area and thought it didn't quite fit in with the elegant layout and décor. It was approximately ten feet square and had only one door that faced the foyer. He realized it must be the monitor room.

"Quite the security set up you have here," Chalmers said, as they walked past the staircase and found themselves in a miniballroom sized room.

"When you are a man in my position and live where I do, you can't be too careful."

Vasquez led them across the miniballroom and through an archway into a large den, decorated with early Victorian furniture and accessories. A large Hispanic man followed the group.

Vasquez turned to Chalmers and said, "Mr. McMillan, I thought our guests would like a cocktail and you and I could talk a little business before dinner."

Chalmers looked at Ian. He nodded and he said, "Go ahead, Dad, we'll be fine."

"Pedro," Vasquez said to the big man, "Would you please tend to our guests and get them what they'd like?"

He motioned to Chalmers who followed him through a door at the far side of the den, into his office and closed the door. He offered Chalmers a chair and moved around to take a seat behind the large oak desk.

Vasquez opened a binder and looked up. His eyes focused on the barrel of the 9mm pistol with attached silencer that Chalmers held, pointed at his head. With an expression of fear and curiosity, he said, "What are you doing? One cry from me and you won't leave this office alive."

"One cry from you and you won't leave this office alive. Now, keep your hands on top of the desk," Chalmers calmly said.

He ordered Vasquez to stand and from behind him with the muzzle of the gun pressed against the back of his head, walked him into an adjoining washroom.

"You can't get away with this. What is it you want?" Vasquez pleaded.

Chalmers pulled a syringe from his jacket pocket and jabbed it into the side of Vasquez's neck.

"I want justice for the slaughter of my neighbor and his family, but you wouldn't understand that," Chalmers said between gritted teeth.

Vasquez turned his incredulous eyes toward Chalmers before they rolled back into his head and he collapsed.

In the den, Dinosa sat her drink on the table beside her and stood up.

She looked sweetly at the large man and said, "El bano, por favor?"

The big man looked at her questioningly and she reiterated, "The ladies room. I need to freshen up."

She pantomimed applying lipstick.

"Ah," the big man said, understanding. "Go through that door," he said pointing, "and la ezquierdo, eh…go left. Two doors, eh, go you right."

"Gracias," Dinosa said and looking at Nancy, added, "Would you care to join me?"

The two women exited the room through the open doorway and turned left.

Steve drained his drink and holding up his empty glass indicated to the big man that he would like a refill. When the man took his glass and turned his back to walk to the bar Nancy and Dinosa slipped back past the doorway and down the hall.

They came to an open door and Nancy peeked in. A young lady was busy arranging place settings at a large dining table. She looked at Dinosa and pulled a small .380 caliper semiautomatic pistol from her evening purse. Dinosa followed suit.

The young lady dropped a fork as she noticed Nancy and Dinosa enter the room. Nancy put her index finger to her lips and said in Spanish, "Shush, we mean you no harm. Just follow instructions."

The young lady, with terrified eyes, nodded. Dinosa gagged and bound her hands behind her. They could hear the clank of pots and pans coming from behind a door at the other side of the room. Escorting the young lady between them they pushed open the door and entered the room.

It was the kitchen. An older woman was bent over in front of the oven. Nancy said, "Pardon me."

The woman stood up holding a pan of freshly baked corn bread which she let go of and it dropped with a clang to the floor.

In Spanish, Nancy said reassuringly, "Please, just do as we say and no harm will come to either of you."

Dinosa walked to the rear of the kitchen and looked out the window. The view was of the outside. She went to a wall switch and flicked it off and on twice.

***

The three men were crouched outside the rear corner of the house in the shadows when they saw the light flash twice from the window above them. Jesse nodded at the other two and still in a crouch ran the twenty yards to the base of the watchtower.

Jeremy made his was to the other end of the house and Grant remained where he was. Jesse slung his rifle over his head and began climbing the spiral ladder. The tower platform lay fifty feet above him. Shod with canvas, rubber soled combat boots, Jesse slowly made his way upwards. Reaching the top, he peeked up and over the manhole entry. Five feet in front of him a man sat on a stool in front of a swivel mounted machine gun. The man's back was to him and he was gazing out onto the estate grounds.

Jesse reached over his left should and grasped the handle of his eight inch combat knife to ensure it was secure, but easy to unsheathe. He placed both palms on either side of the manhole and pushed up and forward. He cleared the manhole and landed just behind the man sitting on the stool.

Startled the man turned and in Spanish said, "What the…"

Jesse snatched his knife from the shoulder sheath and in one motion swiped the blade across the man's neck severing the juggler and the man's trachea. He twisted the man's head away as it gargled, spat a little blood and went limp.

Jesse laid the man's body on floor and took his place on the stool. He looked down and saw Jeremy disappear behind the far corner of the home. Grant was creeping along the near side of the house toward the front. Jesse removed the sling from around his head that was attached to an M24 sniper rifle equipped with a powerful night vision scope.

***

Chalmers opened the office door and said with concern, "Come quickly, something has happened to Senior Vasquez!"

The big man rushed toward the office and made several steps when Chalmers' hand holding the 9mm came from behind his back and shot the big man in the head between his eyes. He dropped with a thud.

He handed the pistol to Ian and retrieved the dead man's gun from his belt holster and handed it to Steve.

"Go," he said to them.

"What about Vasquez?" Steve asked.

"He's fine, now go!"

Steve and Ian crept out of the room and across the ballroom. They were unsure if they would encounter any other body guards. When they reached the foyer, Steve took up a position at the bottom of the stairs and Ian walked to the door of the corner room and knocked.

A sleepy eyed little man that Ian recognized from the night before, sitting with Vasquez in his booth at 'Cabaret del Chapala' and subsequently identified as Pablo's brother Jorge, answered the door. Ian leveled the 9mm at his head and put him back to sleep, forever.

***

Jesse was looking at the two guards chatting and smoking cigarettes at the base of the west wall through his night vision scope. He squeezed the trigger and the silenced weapon pinged as Jesse watched one of the guards head jerk. Before he hit the ground, Jesse had the other man in his sights and squeezed again. The man grabbed his neck and fell. The dog tethered to his wrist bent over and sniffed the dying man.

Realizing his next shot would be considerably longer, Jesse adjusted the sights. He raised the rifle and found his target. He was approaching the other perimeter guard about three hundred meters from Jesse's perch. He squeezed the trigger and an instant later the man toppled. Jesse found his next target as the man reached his partner and bent down. Jesse squeezed the trigger for the fourth time and the man fell across his compadre. The dog, leashed to his wrist, lay down next to him obediently.

From inside the house, Ian opened the front door to the surprise of the guards and shot them both in the head. Grant and Jeremy approached from either side of house, both sliding their bloody knives into their sheaths.

"I take it the house is secured," Grant said.

Ian nodded as Jesse came around the corner and climbed the steps to join the other men. They entered the house and were met by Steve. Nancy and Dinosa were walking toward them accompanied by the cook and the now ungagged and untied maid. Chalmers followed them dragging the still unconscious Vasquez, his hands tied behind him.

Steve tossed a set of keys to his wife who caught them. "These belong to that SUV out front. You can drive these women home after we've secured the front gate. We'll meet you later at the hacienda"

"Let's get this done with," Jesse said, and he, Jeremy and Grant departed in opposite directions. They removed cubes of C4 explosives from their backpacks and planted them   at strategic points in the home and armed them with electronic detonators.

When they returned to the group Ian said, "Okay Nancy, when the shooting stops you can go."

The men carried Vasquez to the van and threw him in the back. They piled in the front, Ian behind the wheel. As they approached the gate, one of the guards was standing in front of it, his automatic pistol at the ready. The other man was standing in the door of the guard shack with a telephone in his hand.

The guard standing in the road held up his hand and yelled, "Alto, alto!"

Ian stopped the van and the man approached the driver side window.

"We have not received permicion for you to leave," he said.

Ian pulled his pistol from his lap and said, "Here's our permicion," and shot him in the head.

From the passenger seat, Grant aimed and shot the other guard. He got out of the van and walked to the shack where he depressed a button and the gate swung open.

Ian pulled the van through and parked off the road. Vasquez stirred in the back and said sleepily, "Where am I?"

A moment later the black SUV pulled up and paused. Through the open window of the passenger seat, Dinosa yelled, "Great party guys, see you back at the house."

They passed Sam driving in the opposite direction in his pick up and waved. Chalmers and Ian were pulling Vasquez from the back of the van when Sam pulled up and stopped.

Vasquez looked at Chalmers with blinking eyes and said, "McMillan, you will die for this."

"I doubt it," Chalmers said, and added, "And my name's not McMillan, it's Chalmers, Chuck Chalmers."

They led Vasquez to the fence wall, blinding him in the headlights of Sam's truck. Sam walked up to the group.

"He's all yours, Sam," Jesse said.

Sam walked over to Vasquez, carrying a razor sharp machete.

Vasquez lowered and turned his head in an effort to see who was standing in front of him and said, "Who, who are you?"

"The name's Sam Francis."

"Do I know you?" Vasquez sniveled.

"No, but you know my daughter, Jaunita. You raped her and had your men drop her in a ditch like she was garbage seven years ago. She was fifteen, do you remember now?"

"No, no senior, it was not me. I couldn't do such a thing," Vasquez pleaded.

"I also knew Alberto Vierra, the late Chief of Police. My kids went to school with his kids and my wife and his wife were friends," Sam spat out.

"Oh Jesus, Son of God," Vasquez prayed, looking toward the heavens.

"You best pray, you son of a bitch, because where you're going you won't see any of them again," Sam bellowed.

He placed the blade of the machete under Vasquez's belt and sliced it in two. His pants fell to his ankles. Sam reached over and pulled his shorts down, revealing his genitals. He grabbed Vasquez's penis and stretched it forward.

"No, no, oh please dear God, no…!" Vasquez screamed, and with one fell sweep Sam severed his manhood from his body.

Vasquez looked down trying to convince himself this was a nightmare. He dropped to his knees and looked up screaming. Sam stuffed the penis in his mouth and took a step back.

With both hand on the machete's handle swung the razor sharp blade and decapitated Vasquez. His head hit the ground with a hollow thud and rolled forward.

Sam lowered his head, dropped the machete and made the sign of the cross.

Jesse walked over and put his arms around Sam and drew him to his body. They stood holding each other for a moment when Sam pushed himself away.

"Jesus Christ, Marine. What kind of chicken shit, lilylivered behavior is this! I wish I could bring that cocksucker back to life and kill him again!" Sam roared.

A moment later Jeremy chuckled and then they were all laughing hysterically. Chalmers walked over and splayed Vasquez's legs out. He picked up the head and posed it between them and said, "That's for you, Dinosa."

He walked over to Sam and retrieving an envelope about an inch thick from his breast pocket, he handed it to Sam.

"This is for you and your family," Chalmers said.

Jesse walked Sam back to his pickup truck and after Sam got in he handed him a set of keys and said, "Happy RVing and boating, the bills of sale are in the whiskey box."

They shook hands and Sam said, "Vios con dios, jar head."

He turned the truck around and headed home.

Jesse, Grant and Jeremy retrieved parachute packs from the back of the van and then said their goodbyes to the rest of the group.

As they walked toward the air strip, Ian said, "See you guys back in Sausalito."

He and the remaining team got in the van and headed back toward 'Hacienda Grande'.

Jesse, Grant and Jeremy walked casually toward the hangar/ warehouse. A gun shot rang out from the darkness inside the building and Jeremy walking in the center of the group, fell to the ground. Jesse and Grant instinctively dropped their parachute pack and dove and rolled on the ground. A bullet whizzed by Grant's head. Coming out of his roll he dashed toward the right side of the door. Just before he reached the cover of the building next to the entrance a bullet found its' mark in his thigh and he tumbled forward.

Jesse was on one knee at the opposite side of the opening and saw the muzzle flash in the darkness. He leveled his 9mm handgun and fired seven or eight rounds, aimed at where he had seen the flash. He crept forward and entered the building. He followed the inside wall until he came to wall box switch.

"Grant, you got cover?" he yelled.

"Yes!"

"Put your glasses on," Jesse yelled.

Several shots rang out and ricocheted above and around Jesse. He reached in his pocket and pulled out a pair of sun glasses and put them on. He reached up and pulled the light switch on.

The entire building suddenly lit up like a stadium at a night football game. Across the room, Grant saw a man behind some barrels with his forearm shielding his eyes from the bright lights and holding a pistol in his other hand.

From the prone position, Grant fired six shots, five of which hit their target. Jesse approached the man cautiously and rolled him over with his foot. He was dead. Jesse looked quickly around the room and determined there were no other shooters.

"Clear!" he roared and rushed to Grant who was sitting up just inside the hangar door.

He was wrapping his wounded leg.

"How bad?" Jesse asked.

"Just a flesh wound, no bone. Go check on Jeremy," Grant grimaced.

Jesse ran out to where Jeremy lay sprawled face down on the ground. He knelt down next to him and gently rolled him over. He was dead. With his head in his lap and rocking, Jesse looked up and wailed, "Oh fuck, Jeremy!"

He stood and picked up the much bigger man and slung him over his massive shoulder and carried him back to the hangar. He passed Grant who was struggling to his feet. Grant said, "Let me give you a hand."

"Just get in the pilot's seat and stay off your feet, I can handle this," Jesse replied.

"What? I can't fly that plane! Jeremy's the pilot," Grant complained.

"Jesus Christ, Grant. You've logged enough hours flying with Jeremy, you ought to be able to fly this thing in your sleep," Jesse retorted.

"Well, I might be able to get her off the ground, but I sure as hell can't land her."

"You fucking moron, you won't have to land it! You'll probably kill us taking off anyhow," Jesse said, shaking his head.

Jesse carried Jeremy, and Grant hobbled over to the door of the twin engine Cessna aircraft. Grant opened the door and pulled himself on board and made his way to the pilot's seat. Jesse laid Jeremy through the door and then jumped over him and pulled him in by his armpits.

"Get this thing started and pull it out of here. I'll meet you on the runway," Jesse said, and grabbed a back pack and exited the plane.

Grant was able to start both engines and nudged the dual throttle control forward. The aircraft inched out of the hangar.

Jesse ran to each corner of the building and planted packs of C4. One corner of the room contained pallets with stacks of flour sacks filled with cocaine. He estimated its' weight at five hundred kilos. He placed an extra pack in that corner.

He ran outside to retrieve their parachute packs and discovered the Cessna was just barely out of the hangar. He ran to the door and opened it. "What the fucks going on?" he yelled above the engine roar.

"I don't know how to steer the son of a bitch. See if you can lift the ass end and turn us!" Grant yelled back.

"Holly shit," Jesse mumbled as he closed the door and walked back to the tail. It took everything he had, but he managed to lift the tail and side step and turned the craft ninety degrees. He followed as Grant eased the plane to the end of the air strip and then Jesse repeated the procedure again to align the plane with the runway.

He ran back and retrieved the parachute bags they had discarded earlier and then back to the plane. He opened the door and boarded the plane. After buckling into the right seat, he crossed himself and said, "Okay Sky King, let's go home."

"Did you see which direction the air sock was going?" Grant asked.

"Why?" Jesse asked.

"Because Jeremy says you're supposed to take off and land going into the wind," Grant exclaimed.

"Jesus Grant, you'll probably crash this son of a bitch before we get off the ground, just go!"

The plane started rumbling down the pavement picking up speed as it went. At about eighty miles per hour, Grant pulled back on the controls and they felt the craft lift off of the ground.

The air strip led out to the open waters of Lake Chapala, for which both men were grateful. Grant banked the plane to the left in an effort to make a uturn and the plane started losing altitude.

"Oh shit," Grant said with a trembling voice. He turned the control to the right and pulled back. The left wing raised about two feet before it would have hit the water. He over compensated and now the right wing was going down. He managed to lift it and the plane began to once again gain altitude. It proceeded on a wig wag course until Grant finally managed to gain control and maintain level flight.

Grant was sweating profusely and Jesse lightened the air, saying, "You couldn't buy a ticket for a better ride than that at Disney World."

Grant managed to get the plane turned around and heading for what he thought would be the Vasquez estate.

"This detonator only has a range of about half a mile, you know," Jesse said.

"I know, I know," Grant replied, "That has to be it dead ahead."

They saw the brightly lit grounds the Valdez home ahead and just off to their left. Grant lowered the nose and turned the plane so it passed over the home at five hundred feet elevation. Jesse threw the switch on the remote detonator.

Ten seconds later the night lit up as first the house and then the warehouse blew up in an inferno of fire. When the smoke settled both buildings were leveled.

"Keep her under the radar and head west," Jesse said smiling.

***

Chalmers had a golf bag slung over one shoulder and was carrying an overnight bag and pulling a suitcase on wheels down the walkway from the entrance to 'Hacienda Grande' towards the van. A flash of red light lit up the horizon in front of him to the east. He stopped and watched in amazement.

Coming down the stairs behind him, Dinosa stopped and whistled. "Holy shit!" she marveled.

Two consecutive loud booms followed and echoed around the hills behind them.

"Nothing like the smell of hot C4 in the morning," Steve said, standing next to Ian at the rear of the van.

The group made one more trip retrieving their belongings from the house and loaded them into the van before everybody filed in. As they pulled away from 'Hacienda Grande', Chalmers glanced at his watch. It read 3:15 am.

As the wheels of the Cessna Citation lifted off the runway at Guadalajara Airport, Chalmers looked at his watch again. It read 6:05 am. He reclined his seat, closed his eyes and reflected over the events of the last few days.

It was hard for him to believe that the team had landed on this same runway less than five days ago. Events and scenes would play back in slow motion in his mind and speed up in a jerky motion and skip back and forth as if someone was controlling it with a remote DVD controller. He finally dosed off into a deep sleep.

Dinosa was shaking him gently when he woke.

"We're on final approach. Drop your cock and grab your sock, soldier," she said with a laugh.

Chalmers brought his seat upright and said with a smile, "Thank you, sergeant."

When he looked down and out of the window he saw the waters of the San Francisco Bay. He felt relieved.

After the plane landed it taxied to the private international arrival area and parked. The team debarked and was led across the tarmac and into the arriving passenger building. After they passed through customs and immigration they waited in baggage area.

From across the room they heard someone yell, "Daddy."

Chalmers turned around and saw Jenifer running towards him. Behind her in a group were Colleen and Sheila and her two children, Matthew and Shannon.

When Jennifer reached her father she jumped up and wrapped her arms around his neck and said tearfully, "Oh Dad, we were so worried."

Chalmers sat her down on her feet and said, dumbfounded, "Why? Nobody ever got hurt on a golf course."

The rest of the welcoming home group joined the team and hugs were shared all around.

Colleen and Chalmers kissed and held their embrace. Finally Colleen pulled her head back, looked up at her husband

and said, "The next time you decide to go south of the border, we're coming with you."

***

"God, I hope Jeremy was right. He said with the wing tanks and auxiliary fuel tanks topped off, we should have a range maximum of about 1,800 miles. That'll put us in the drink somewhere between Los Angeles and San Francisco," Jesse said, looking at a map unfolded on his lap.

They were approaching the east coast of Baja California over the Gulf of California.

"Once we've cleared Baja, I'll put us in a down glide path. We're at eight thousand feet now and that should conserve some fuel. Just think happy thoughts," Grant said.

"You know, your fucking optimistic attitude is really starting to get to me. Like that op we had off the coast of Somalia and we were surrounded by militia gun boats and you said…"

They continued to talk old war stories for the next several hours. They were ten mile off the coast of California and had passed San Diego and Los Angeles. Suddenly they heard the right engine cough.

"Oh shit," Grant groaned and threw the fuel switch from auxiliary tank back to wing tanks.

Jesse grabbed the radio microphone and said, "Tonto to Lone Ranger, over."

They waited for an agonizing amount of time. Grant started wagging the plane back and forth.

"What are you doing that for?" Jesse asked, incredulously.

"I don't know. I saw it in a movie once," Grant replied.

"Ah shit, there you go with that optimistic attitude again."

The speaker crackled and they heard, "Tonto this is the Lone Ranger. What's your twenty, over?"

"Approximately two hundred fifty miles north of Los Angeles, ten miles off the coast. I think I can see Santa Cruz, over," Grant said.

Jesse unbuckled and jumped to the rear of the plane. He unlatched the door which opened like a hatch, going out and up. They had put their parachute packs on hours earlier and he also rigged Jeremy to a pack with a ten foot static line. He dragged Jeremy over next to the door.

"Tonto this is the Lone Ranger. We have you insight. We're slightly west about one mile north of you, over"

Both engines suddenly sputtered and died. Grant yelled, "Go, go!" and Jesse pushed Jeremy's body out of the door and followed. Grant was a step behind them and he jumped out.

They were at one thousand feet above the Pacific Ocean when they bailed out of the plane. Both men immediately deployed their chutes and directed themselves toward Jeremy, who was drifting away from the coast. They watched as the airplane plunged into the water and almost immediately sink less than a mile away.

They splashed down within ten yards on either side of their dead comrade and unbuckled their harnesses. They swam over and unbuckled Jeremy's harness and each held an arm as the three bobbed in the ocean.

Five minutes later Sean maneuvered the stern of his sixty foot yacht to within twenty feet of the men and killed the engines. Garcia was standing on the aft swim platform and pulled Jeremy's lifeless body up and then onto the deck. He turned and assisted Grant and Jesse on board.

Garcia knelt down beside Jeremy and made of the sign of the cross. Looking up at the sad faces of Grant and Jesse, he said, "What happened?" and immediately regretted it and quickly added, "Never Mind."

Sean restarted the engines and set a heading back to San Francisco Bay and the Port of Sausalito.

***

Doctor Zacharias Peterson, Chief Medical Examiner of the Marin County Coroners Office, stood next to a gurney on the dock at the Sausalito Marina and watched as the yacht named after his late sister and the wife of Sean O'Farrell, 'Louan' maneuvered into its' space and Jesse tied the mooring lines to the pier's deck cleats.

Sean climbed down from the fly bridge and stepped onto the dock. He walked directly to Doctor Peterson and they shook hands.

"Zack, it's good to see you. I wish it were under better circumstances."

"Anything for my favorite brotherinlaw," Zack said.

"I know I'm asking you to go above and beyond what I deserve. You certainly deserve an explanation and I promise you one day you'll get it," Sean said, apologetically.

"What do you mean? Like you said on the phone, diving accidental drownings happen all the time," Zack remarked.

"Thanks, I'll make sure that you get his birth certificate and affidavits from all of us. He had no known family so would you see that his body gets to the Sausalito Crematory and Funeral Home and tell Saul Holtzman I'm taking care of the expenses?"

"No problem," Zack said.

Chapter Twenty-One

The ocean was unusually calm as the 'Louan' cruised under the Golden Gate Bridge and out of the San Francisco Bay and into the Pacific Ocean. To her rear the sun was rising above the east bay hills and in front of her the skies were clear and free of the morning fog bank that usually blanketed the coast. Even the waters of the infamous 'potato chop' where the bay met the ocean and were known to be at times lethally heavy, were today calm.

The three youngsters, Jennifer, Shannon and Matthew, sat cross legged on her bow breathing in the fresh salty air.

Sean sat at the helm in the fly bridge, joined now by Chalmers and Colleen.

Chalmers sat down in the captain's chair next to Sean and Colleen stood in front of him with his arms wrapped around her, both looking out at the ocean's horizon.

"Couldn't have asked more a more beautiful day," Chalmers said.

"How's everybody doing?" Sean asked.

"As well as can be expected, I guess," Chalmers replied and added, "Those are some amazing young people."

Sean glanced at his watch. It read 5:55 am.

"It's time," he said and pulled the throttle back and cut the engines.

The three joined the group on the aft deck, as did the three youngsters. Nancy, Steve, and Ian were clad in Navy dress uniforms and Jesse in his Marine blues.

Nancy lifted the urn from the table and moved to the leeward side of the boat. Her three mates followed her. The three men stood at attention and as a bugled 'Taps' began to play on the boat's loudspeaker, they saluted smartly. Nancy removed the urn's lid and began emptying its' contents. She turned and handed the urn to her husband and stood beside the others and saluted.

This solemn procedure continued until Jesse emptied the urn's contents. He turned and faced his comrades and the group behind him. With the urn under his arm he saluted.

When 'Taps' concluded he said, "At ease."

"Jeremy Earl Colt was a proud Marine," Jesse started. "He was an orphan and some said he had no family. I beg to differ. He had a large family and some of this brothers and sisters are gathered here today.

"I've been asked by our family to say a few words. I'm not very good at this, but last night I got some heartfelt advice from a young lady."

He looked at Jennifer and smiled.

"There is no reason why a person dies, the important thing is why he lived. Here are the reasons I believe Jeremy Earl Colt lived…"

THE END
BOOK ONE

Epilogue

The Hope

There's a town called Hope in Northern Idaho. It sits on the northern shore of Lake Pend Orielle in the pan handle. I think it got its' name by the early settlers who said, "I hope we can make it through this winter."

Valerie Kane sat at the table in the corner at Lefty's Tavern, playing with the swizzle stick in the cocktail glass in front of her. Ms. Kane was the former San Francisco County Assistant District Attorney originally assigned to the George Spinella case. She had since resigned her position to accept the job as a prosecuting attorney with the U.S. Justice Department. She was a pretty and petite blonde in her late thirties and because of her innocent appearance was often underestimated by her peers and adversaries. She was a hardnosed proven prosecutor.

Dinosa and Chalmers entered the tavern together and seeing Kane they walked to her table.

As they pulled up chairs, she greeted them, "Mary, Chuck, so good to see you again. Thank you for agreeing to meet me."

"Nice to see you too," Dinosa said and continued, "Let's cut the niceties and get down to it. What's on your mind, Val?"

"That's one of the things I admire about you, Inspector Dinosa. You pull no punches," Kane chuckled.

Chalmers smiled and said, "Valerie, speaking for myself, it's good to see you and congratulations on your new position,"

"Thank you both, and I will get right to the point. I'm the lead government prosecutor on the Luke Watson case. Off the record I'd like to ask you what you know," Kane said.

"What makes you think either of us knows anything?" Chalmers asked coyly.

"Oh come on. Don't treat me like your sixth grade substitute teacher," Kane said and continued, "I already told you this conversation is off the record."

Dinosa looked at Chalmers and then back at Kane. "Suppose we were to tell you, you should look higher than Watson?"

Kane raised an eye brow and said, "I'm listening."

***

Sean sat behind his desk across from Garcia.

"What's on your mind, John?"

"Well, first I think based on conversations we've had before, you knew I would be requesting this meeting," Garcia started.

After Sean nodded, he proceeded, "I also believe that you and several other members of this team are aware that the corruption goes beyond Luke Watson. Based on the information Grub has gathered I think he's produced more questions than answers.

"I know the inner workings and the hierarchy at the DEA and I have resources outside the agency in Arlington, but I can't pursue an investigation on my own.

"I don't know how your foundation works and I don't need to know. I'm asking that it get involved. I need your resources."

***

Grub and his fiancée, Belinda Grant, better known as Snoops or Snoopy to her friends, sat snuggled on the love seat swing on the lanai of their rental beach cottage in Princeville, Kauai, Hawaii. This had become his favorite island resort and he was delighted to share it with the one he loved.

Grub and Snoopy had met each other about a year earlier. Snoopy was an IT with the San Francisco Police Department and was working on the George Spinella case when Grub was brought in as a consultant.

"Ya know Snoops," he said, pulling her closer, "This kinda sucks having to meet here once a year. I mean, since I started my own company I can live wherever I want. I'm tired of Boise, Idaho. I like the Santa Cruz Mountains. What do you think?"

Belinda looked up at him and trying not to sound too excited, said, "I think that'd be great. We would certainly live closer to one another."

"I was also thinking I'm gonna have a lot of work and will probably need a partner. What'ya say?"

"Wow, let me think about that," Belinda said and then quickly added, "Okay."

***

BOOK TWO

Los Santos

PART I

The Slaughter

"Son, you don't know what slaughter is."
My father's response when I told him my high school
football team got slaughtered by our cross town rival.

Chapter One

Cochise County Sheriff Edwardo Jimenez kissed his wife, Marlene, at the front door of their ranch home, located just west of the southern border town of Douglas, Arizona.

"Wish us luck," he said, grabbing his uniform Stetson off the hat rack.

The sheriff knew he would need more than luck. He had started his crusade six months earlier, visiting rallies and local council meetings in towns throughout the county. He had first hand accounts of the atrocities carried out by the drug cartels and the so called 'war on drugs' declared by his own government.

He didn't need to research the 'war on drugs', he had lived it. For every battle won there were literally dozens lost. Just the week before a drug cartel war had spilled over from the Mexican town of Aqua Prieta into the streets of Douglas. The carnage had resulted in the deaths of twenty people in Aqua Prieta and nine people in Douglas, including three children and one of his deputies. A total of four victims could be traced to rival drug cartel members, battling over control of their product since the death of Pablo Vasquez, leader of the 'El Diablo' cartel. The other dead were innocent bystanders.

One of the more pathetic outcomes was the fact that three weapons recovered after the slaughter could be traced back to the ATF's 'Operation Fast and Furious'. He asked himself, what idiot came up with that plan and even more idiotic, what bureaucratic moron had okayed it.

The only positive outcome of the slaughter was the national attention that ensued. He had been interviewed by the national

152 D. Patrick Carroll

media outlets and he let his opinion be known. He believed the nation should legalize drugs.

He remembered the look of total distain on the network news woman's face when she asked him, "Let me get this right, you would legalize the drugs that are decimating our children and bringing death and destruction to our streets?"

"I'm saying I would legalize something that has and will continue to decimate our society and bring even more death and destruction to not only our streets, but streets around the world, especially in Mexico.

"You are one of the millions of Americans that sit in your plush homes and don't give a damn what havoc these drugs and their distribution networks bring, as long as it doesn't directly affect you. You are part of the problem.

"Let me ask you, would you even be here if this atrocity had happed only in Agua Prieta, Mexico?"

There were no follow up questions asked.

Now he was heading to Tucson to meet with a state legislator and other citizens of like mind and fly to Washington, D.C., to testify before the Congressional Judicial Oversight Committee.

He got into his County Sheriff's Bronco and turned the ignition on. The concussion of the blast blew Marlene back from the open doorway where she had stood seeing her husband off, into the living room landing her behind a couch, protecting her from the Bronco debris and flying glass that followed.

She could hear nothing but a high pitched ringing in her ears. She crawled to the doorway and looked out. She remembered seeing smoke and the frame of the Bronco crumpled in her front yard before she passed out.

***

Chapter Two

Charles Raymond Chalmers passed through the security gate and drove up the lane and through the grounds of the Armstrong estate. He was thinking about the incredible journey that had brought him to this place.

He was born and raised in San Francisco, the city he loved. His father was a street beat cop on the SFPD in a time when the term 'flat foot' had literal meaning. His dad walked a beat. It was a time when a cop knew almost everyone on his route, from the corner butcher to the little old lady that lived in the second story flat on the corner that he would help by carrying her groceries.

Hell, only one in three households owned an automobile. Chalmers grew up living with his parents and older brother and sister on Polk Street in the City's North Beach District. Almost everything a family needed was within a three block walk. Within that three block perimeter was the corner market, the barber shop, the pharmacy with a soda fountain, the café, two neighborhood pubs and the public elementary school. Even the family doctor was only four blocks away on Van Ness Avenue.

Chalmers had seen the world change. He had enlisted in the Army after he graduated from Balboa high School and was trained as a military policeman. Upon returning after a three year hitch he attended City College before 'forensic science' was in the vocabulary.

He attended the Police Academy and realized one of his life's dreams, becoming a rookie policeman in 1981.

Now, here he was thirty something years later about to meet with some people who had only one thing in common, other than being incredibly rich. They were surviving family members of women murdered over two years ago by the same psychopathic killer. He wondered what route this journey would now take him.

Chalmers was escorted to the den inside the 'Armstrong Castle'. The home's name was coined by its affluent neighbors residing in the Los Gatos Hills after George Armstrong and his siblings failed attempt to convert the estate into a historical museum for the news media after the death of their mother. The name stuck and the estate became a local landmark.

Sean and Ian O'Farrell had not yet arrived, but the other two trustees were present, George Armstrong and Sol Goldsmith, along with John Garcia, the presenter of today's proposal. Chalmers was surprised to see Belinda 'Snoopy' Grant and her fiancé Doctor Daniel 'Grub' Tanaka.

Snoopy got up from the settee she was sharing with Grub and rushed over and greeted Chalmers with a hug. He shook Grub's hand and said, "I heard you two were an item, congratulations. What brings you here?"

Grub responded, "We've been working with John and have dug up some interesting things. He wanted us here to support his proposal and share our initial findings."

"Well, it's good to see you both," Chalmers said, sitting down in an easy chair next to them.

"Sorry we're late," Sean said as he and Ian entered the room.

"Good to see you," Armstrong said, "I believe everyone's here so let's get started. John, you have the floor."

John Garcia stood next to a wall mounted large flat screen television. The furniture in the room had been rearranged so that everyone faced him.

"You may think the first images you're about to see are a dramatic attempt to shock and disgust you. You would be right," Garcia started.

Still images began flashing on the big screen. They showed scenes of carnage, of sometimes mass mutilated bodies and sometimes single bodies of dead young children.

Pictures of burned out buildings and devastated villages and blown up cars with debris littering the streets flashed on the screen. Some of the scenes depicted sobbing survivors and others of funeral processions with people carrying multiple caskets.

Garcia, who had remained silent through the slide presentation, said, "These pictures were taken on both sides of the border. In Mexico, through fear and intimidation the drug cartels have taken over entire States. Their influence permeates the national political structures and threatens to take over the entire nation.

"We discovered during 'Operation Montezuma's Revenge', that this corruption has now pervaded our government, to what extent? I'll let Doctor Tanaka tell you in a minute.

"Most of you are successful business people. Let me ask you, how would you like to own a business that returned more than a five hundred percent profit on your investment? Add to that, you have an almost unlimited demand for your product and a continuous supply."

A colored pie chart appeared on the screen. The pie represented the estimated five hundred billion dollar international illegal drug trade. The pie was yellow with a tiny slice of red. The red represented one half of one percent of the pie and the amount of drugs confiscated by various law agencies.

"How many retail companies would love to say they lost only one half of one percent of the gross to theft, spoilage or damage?" Garcia asked rhetorically.

He continued, "We all know that charts and statistics can prove elephants fly. My point here is, this pie represents a whole lot of ill gotten gains. It represents more money than ninety percent of the world's nation's gross domestic product.

"We all know money, especially corrupt money creates corrupt power. How much money are these animals willing to pay and how far does the corruption extend? I don't know, but Grub and Snoops have done some digging into Pablo Vasquez's finances and have discovered some interesting trails."

He pointed to Grub and nodded.

"During 'Operation Montezuma's Revenge'," Grub started, "John asked me to see what I could come up with regarding the finances of Pablo Vasquez and the 'El Diablo' Cartel and it appears most of the drug income was diverted to a Mexican company Vasquez owns, or since his untimely death I should say owned, called 'Las Exportar'.

"We started reading their corporate ledger going back one year and it's hard to tell how much of their revenue came from the cartel, but I'd estimate over the past year approximately fortyfive billion came from the cartel.

"Their internal books showed a cash slush fund account that carried an average balance of about ten million dollars. Checks from that account in amounts ranging from ten thousand to half a million dollars were written to Pablo Vasquez or his brother Jorge to cover personal business related expenses. Over the past year about fifty million was dispersed from that fund.

"We also traced bank transfers that totaled about sixty billion dollars to an account in a Swiss bank. It appears to be an investment account in a Greek corporation called 'Free the World Investments'.

"We've been able to determine that George Aristotle owns the majority of that corporation's stock, but it appears he holds no position on the board nor is he a corporate officer.

"The corporate charter calls itself a for profit company that invests in third world countries to promote economic freedom and security. That appears to be complete bull shit. We found no such investments."

George Armstrong interrupted and asked, "Have you been able to follow any of the disbursements made by 'Free the World Investments'?"

"Snoops and I are trying to crack that nut now and we're getting close," Grub responded and added, "I know all of this can be a little confusing, but we've compiled a written report and you will all get a copy. We make no conclusions. We leave that up to you."

"Thank you, Grub," Garcia said and continued, "The conclusion I've come to and it is my hope you will too, is that the war on drugs has failed. The war that America has waged to save the poor miserable bastard that wastes away on our streets getting high has not only failed him, but has become instrumental in his growing numbers.

"As you all know I was a DEA field agent. I spent time on the front lines of this war. Myself, as well as thousands of other dedicated men and women have put our lives on the line and we have seen first hand the devastating effects of what the drug runners were doing and we fought that war. We have been in the jungles of Columbia and Bolivia and the streets of Mexican villages and our own cities.

"And now the enemy has declared war not only on the ones that would fight to interdict their filthy lucre, but the ones who would campaign to end its illegality. If that ever happened it would kill their cash cow.

"Just yesterday, a courageous County Sheriff in southeast Arizona was blown to bits in his own yard in front of his wife because he had the balls to advocate what he knew to be the truth.

"We called 'Operation Montezuma's Revenge' a success. We accomplished the mission. We avenged the senseless slaughter of a San Francisco family. We rid the world of one of its' most evil citizens, but that resulted in more slaughter by creating a void and allowing other, just as evil people, to take his place. No matter how many battles we may win, we cannot win this war. We have to admit it.

"I haven't even touched on our nation's drug production and distribution. Legalizing drugs would almost overnight shut down the thousands of garage and backyard meth and ecstasy labs. It would cut the funds to gangs and their distribution network that are a cancer to our inner cities and consume such a large portion of our law enforcement resources.

"I ask you to think also of the monetary rewards legalizing drugs would create. If done in a responsible way, we could tax the sales. By selling it in a sterile environment we would create legal employment for thousands and the addict wouldn't be sharing needles or being the victim of contaminated drugs and paraphernalia.

"A conservative survey concludes that over seventy percent of the persons incarcerated in our jails and prisons have been convicted of drug related crimes. What kind of madness is this?

"The inner city 'turf' gangs are not some kind of a modern day 'Robin Hood and his Merry Men' protecting their neighborhoods. They're punks protecting their drug income."

Garcia paused to allow his audience time to absorb what he had said.

He continued, "I believe this group has the resources to greatly contribute to putting an end to this madness. If we use our investigative and operational potential we can provoke public opinion to change the laws and end this holocaust.

"Simply legalizing all drugs would, of course be ludicrous. Laws would have to be put in place to control the sales and the buyers. Driving under the influence of drugs that would impair a person's ability to drive safely, for instance would be unacceptable, but we already have laws in place. Safe and halfway houses would have to be expanded in numbers and counseling as well.

"The main target for changing our laws should be aimed at those who currently profit from the illegal sales and cause so much havoc and destruction to our society. We need to put these bastards out of business.

"That, gentlemen, is my proposal," He concluded.

"Let me make sure I have this right," Sol Goldsmith said. "If your proposal was successfully carried out, it would result in the legalization of all drugs and that, in and by itself, would end the corruption and carnage."

"Sol, the criminal element will always be with us. When our government lifted prohibition on liquor it did not result in creating more alcoholics. It took the criminal element out of it and resulted in a drastic reduction of crime in our streets. Sure, organized crime resorted to other illegal activities, but the blood baths in the streets of Chicago and New York and other major cities decreased drastically. Believe me, the mafia was not happy with the end of prohibition.

"What I'm saying is we could do the same thing to the drug cartels. There would no longer be the endless stream of money for payoffs to corrupt officials or rival gang and cartel hit squads to murder each other and any innocents that may get in the way."

Chalmers asked, "If what you say is true about the second front of this war is to eliminate

those who would campaign to legalize drugs and we agreed to accept your proposal, don't you think everyone in this room and our families would be at risk?"

"Chuck, I have asked myself and continue to ask myself that same question and in a word the answer is yes. Every action we take, if you agree to undertake this proposal, must be taken with complete secrecy. One misstep or leak could end in a fiasco. I for one am willing to take that chance," Garcia stated.

"Have you developed a plan of action?" Ian asked.

"Yes, but it's basic and preliminary and I was hoping, after you've had a chance to review it, with your input, together we could hone it," Garcia replied.

"Let me suggest," Sean said, "we all take the time to review this material and consider John's proposal and meet back here the day after tomorrow."

***

Chapter Three

Ara Ceros sat at the head of the conference table pouring scalding water into his cup, blending it with the strong Turkish coffee bean powder. Three other men sat around the table located in the conference room on the top floor of the Platia Kotzia Building in the financial district of Athens, Greece.

"The boss is not happy," he began and continued, "The reports we are receiving tell us since the death of Pablo Vasquez, the battle for his business has been fierce and is spilling over into the United States. This is not good for our business."

He looked sternly at the men sitting around him.

"Mr. Ceros, if I may," said Kevin Whitehead, an Englishman in his mid forties and a senior vicepresident of 'Free the World Investments'.

He went on, "Our people in Mexico tell us there are two warring factions vying for that business. One is comprised of remnant factions of the 'El Diablo' cartel. They seem to be disorganized and scrambling to maintain relations with our Columbian partners. The other group is the Morales group, better known as the 'Mexican Mafia'. Eric Morales has a vast distribution network in place in the U.S. and the Columbians say they can work with him.

"The only concern by our man in Mexico is whether Morales can work with the government connections we've established. I think he can be persuaded it would be in his best interest to cooperate with our directions."

Ceros thought for a moment and then said, "It sounds like the Morales cartel will be our new partner. Kevin, I'm putting you in charge of settling the dispute. See to it that no more bloodshed spills over into the United States, and see if you can change the name 'Mexican Mafia', it sounds so barbaric."

Whitehead nodded and cleared his throat, "Mr. Ceros, there seems to be a more pressing problem with this portion of our business. There's a growing movement in the States to legalize drugs. If that movement is successful, I'm sure you can understand what a tremendous effect it would have on our cash flow.

"We don't know who authorized or perpetrated it, but yesterday morning a local American Sheriff from Arizona was assassinated. He was on his way to testify before the U.S. Congress on behalf of those who would legalize drugs.

"If the idea gets out that the drug cartel had this man killed to protect the illegality of their trade, it would be like adding fuel to the fire."

"We can't have that," Ceros bellowed. "Make sure we use all of our resources to make sure that doesn't happen. Get to the bottom of who was responsible and eliminate them. I also want you to present a plan of action to subvert this so called growing movement."

"Does that mean," Whitehead asked, "I can pressure our political and media friends in the United States?"

"I said use all of our assets, just make sure it can't be traced back to us," Ceros said and added, "Speaking of tracing it back to us, tell me about that idiot DEA official the FBI arrested."

"Let's just say, that problem is being handled," Whitehead said.

***

"Hey Mary, it's Chuck," Chalmers said into his phone.

"Ah shit, why do I always feel like grabbing my ankles whenever you call me Mary," Dinosa groaned.

"Come on Dinosa, I'm just calling you to congratulate you on your new job," Chalmers said with a chuckle.

"Yeah, right, I'm still bent over," she sneered.

"Seriously, how does it feel to be on the Justice Department payroll? How are things going?" Chalmers asked.

Mary Dinosa had recently accepted a position of Special Investigator with the U.S. Attorney General's Office as an aid to Prosecutor Valerie Kane.

"Hell, I've only been on the job two weeks," she replied.

"I was thinking, maybe we could get together and share notes. How about Lefty's tonight?" Chalmers said hopefully.

"Here it comes. I've braced myself," Mary cynically said.

"I'm serious Mary," he said and added, "I have some information you can use and should know."

"Okay Chuck, but don't get the idea we'll be sharing warm midnight showers anytime soon. See you at fivethirty."

***

"It has to be done soon," Whitehead said into his phone and continued, "And it has to be done fast. We want no publicity from this, comprende?"

"Si, Senior Whitehead, I understand. The meeting is already set up. In less than one hour our problem will be resolved," Paulo Mendoza said.

"Good," Whitehead said hanging up.

Mendoza walked from his office to his den and prepared for the upcoming meeting, A half hour later his assistant came to the door and said, "Senior Mendoza, your guests have arrived."

"Good, ask them to join me."

Three Hispanic men were escorted into the den. Paulo rose to greet them and smiling, said in Spanish, "Welcome, I have good news. Please sit down."

The three men took chairs in front of the fireplace and Paulo filled four glasses on the coffee table with tequila and handed a glass to each man. Raising his glass he said, "Viva El Diablo," and emptied his glass with a swallow.

The other men raised their glasses and in unison said, "Viva El Diablo," and slammed their shots down.

The man to Paulo's left started, "So what..." and then grasped his throat and started to gag. The other men did the same. One by one they toppled onto the floor and jerked in violent seizures. Less than a minute later they were dead.

Paulo summoned his assistant and said, "Get some help and take these three out at least five miles into the desert and bury them and get rid of their car. Take some pictures before you bury them."

***

"Over here Chuck," Chalmers heard as walked into Lefty's Tavern, blinking his eyes trying to adjust to the dim light after coming in from the bright sunshine outside. He caught sight of a silhouetted arm waving in the corner.

He walked clumsily toward the figure and as he got closer he recognized Dinosa and saw another woman sitting across from her with her back toward him. Approaching the table he said, "Mary, good to see you," and recognizing the other woman added, "and, ah, you too Valerie."

"Don't look so surprised. You didn't think I'd keep any secrets from my boss, did you?" Dinosa said.

"No, actually I 'm glad you're here Valerie. I should have included you in my invitation, you should hear what I have to say."

"Well, let's hear it," Dinosa said.

"I understand you're the lead prosecutor in the Luke Watson case. We have reason to believe his life is in danger. Do you remember when Mary and I told you to look higher up the food chain after his arrest?"

Kane looked at Dinosa and nodded.

Chambers continued, "We haven't been able to connect all the dots, but we believe an international corporation, "Save the World Investments' is financing payoffs to politicians and government officials in this country.

"Are you willing to go wherever this investigation takes it?" he asked.

"Yes," Kane said offensively and continued, "We are absolutely aware of the threat on Watson's life and he's currently being held in protective solitary confinement at San Quentin. He's of course not talking to us, but we're sweating him out with multiple murder and treason charges and have made overtures to his counsel of a possible plea arrangement.

"We conducted a search of his office and home and found about eighty thousand dollars in his home safe along with a phony passport. We've also discovered a numbered offshore bank account in his name, but because of international banking laws we haven't been able to access it."

"If I could get that account number, we might be able to access it for you," Chalmers said.

"Fucking Grub, I should've known," Dinosa said, rubbing the top of her head.

"That would be against the ethic of my office," Kane said deviously, "but there may be ways. Let me think about that."

"Both of you please be very careful. We know we're dealing with some very dangerous people, maybe some in your own department. I wouldn't trust anyone."

Kane looked across the table into Chalmers eyes and said, "Don't worry so much Chuck. Even my boss thinks we're conducting a routine investigation and prosecution of Luke Watson for murder conspiracy in the deaths of the Barnes family. Any information that we share or may find out about involvement from 'up the food chain' will stay between us until the time is right and if that time should come I promise to give you fair warning," Kane said.

"Sounds good," Chalmers said rising to leave.

"Tell Ian O'Farrell I said hi and to call me sometime," Dinosa said with a wink.

***

"Jesus Max, I'm fucked," Luke Watson said, running his hand across his face and nervously tapping a heel on the floor beneath his chair.

He sat across the table from his lawyer, Maxwell Snyder, in the Attorney/Convict conference room at San Quentin Prison.

Watson was a senior at Cornell University when Snyder pledged his fraternity as a freshman. They had not been close, but Watson knew he had gone on to become one of the best defense attorneys in the world, and he was a fraternity brother.

"Listen Luke, I've convinced the judge to convene a bail request hearing and I believe that will happen soon. I know it's tough in here, but just hang in there and say nothing to anyone."

"What are our chances he'll grant bail?" Watson asked anxiously.

"That depends on how strong the prosecutor's case is. All I know right now are the charges filed against you. Frankly, it doesn't look good," Snyder said and then continued, "What would you say if I approached the prosecutor with a deal proposal?"

"What do you mean?" Watson asked, leaning forward.

Snyder cleared his throat and said, "Well, if I could convince her that you have provable information that could land her bigger fish, she may be willing to deal."

"What kind of a deal could we make?"

Snyder looked at him curiously and said, "That depends on what you could tell them. It could be anywhere from reduced charges to dismissal of all charges and your release into the Federal Witness Protection Program."

"What if I could lead them to top agency officials within the President's Administration?" Watson said looking at him hopefully, and then added, "And how about overseas influence buying?"

"That sounds tempting. Let me see what I can do?" Snyder said, standing up.

"Oh God, Max, if you could get me out of this I would be eternally grateful," Watson said, standing up and pumping his hand.

"Hey, it's just one Phi Beta Kappa doing for another brother," Snyder said before calling for the jailer.

Once he had driven off the prison grounds, Snyder pulled over to the side of the road and dialed a number on his cell phone.

"Mr. Whitehead, please," he said.

***

Sean, Ian and Garcia pulled into the circular driveway and parked below the O'Farrell estate in the hills overlooking Sausalito and the San Francisco Bay. As they trudged up the steps to the house they were met by a parade of people coming down, led by Sheila Lamont followed by Donelda Garcia and her two sons, John Jr. and Robert and Sheila's children Matthew and Shannon.

"Hi honey, where are you guys off to?" Sean asked as they met.

"Hi Dad," she said and answered, "We're going to the City and meet up with Colleen and Jennifer and the do a little sightseeing. We'll probably go to Golden Gate Park and the De Young Museum, maybe we'll go to the Zoo.

"Well have a good time," Sean said.

"Oh, by the way, we'll be catching dinner in San Francisco, so you boys are on your own, tata."

"Aw God, why do I get the feeling pizza's on the menu tonight," Ian said, feigning distaste.

The three men continued up the steps and entered the mansion. Sean and Garcia went directly to Sean's office and Ian found their other two house guests out back lounging by the swimming pool nursing a beer. He opened the cooler door in the patio bar and pulled a cold beer from the ice.

Standing on the deck, he yelled down to the two men, "Hey guys, why don't you join me?"

Grant Wilson and Jesse Leone struggled off their lounges and came up onto the deck and sat down joining Ian at a table under the awning

"How'd it go?" Grant asked, as Ian handed them both a fresh beer.

"Well, it looks like your life of Riley is about to be disturbed," Ian said.

"What are we going to be doing?" Jesse asked.

Ian marveled at his military way of thinking. It was never why, it was always what.

"I'm not sure yet," Ian answered and continued, "He wants the foundation to lead the 'legalize drug' campaign, and has some compelling arguments. I'm not sure what our roles will be."

Sean walked out onto the deck carrying an armful of folders and interrupted, "Maybe this will explain it better."

He handed each man a folder and taking a chair said, "This is a copy of John's proposal. I'd like all of us to read it and we can discuss it afterwards."

Fifteen minutes into the reading, Jesse looked up and exclaimed, "Holy crap, I think I knew this Sheriff Jimenez, or should I say I know his son, Joe."

The other men looked at him curiously and Grant asked, "What are you talking about, Jesse.."

"I was born and raised in Douglas, Arizona. I went through school with Joe. I think he was a grade or two behind me and we weren't great friends, but hell, we played on the same high school football team. His father was the County Sheriff ever since I can remember."

"Small world ain't it?" Ian said, "You might have just found one of our roles in this."

***

"Holy Moly!" Grub yelled, "Come look at this."

Snoops hadn't seen Grub this excited since they had broken the password on George Spinella's lap top. She got up from her desk and walked over to where Grub sat.

Looking over his shoulder, she asked, "What?"

Chuck gave me this account number from Luke Watson's Cayman Island bank and I was able to trace the deposits back to their origin. It wasn't easy but I found a back door and voila, I'm in the 'Save the World Investments' computer system.

"I'm gonna log you in. Download their operational files and I'll get their financial information. Hurry, we need to get this before they detect us and shut us down," Grub exclaimed.

***

The board of directors of the 'Justice Foundation' met in the same room they had convened in two days earlier.

"Based on the late information Grub and Snoopy have provided and the upgraded proposal with strategies, I recommend we accept it and proceed," Sol Goldsmith said.

The motion was duly seconded by George Armstrong and unanimously passed.

Ian grabbed Chalmers by his upper arm and said, "Chuck, we have to talk."

Later that afternoon Chalmers found himself in the company of Ian, Grant and Jesse inside the cabin of the O'Farrell Company's Cessna Citation Jet as is departed San Francisco International Airport.

Jesse was on his cell phone saying, "Joe Jimenez?...Yes this is Jesse Leone...Yes that Jesse Leone...It's good to talk to you too. I'd like to say how sorry I am to learn about your father...Well, that's why I'm calling. I can't really discuss it over the phone, but a few friends of mine and I are heading to Douglas now and it's kind of important that we meet with you...Seven, tonight?...That sounds great, see you then."

Jesse turned to his traveling companions and said, "It's all set. We're meeting Joe at a bar called 'Bailey's' tonight at seven."

***

Chapter Four

"How in the hell could this happen?!" George Aristotle roared.

He was sitting in a rattan lounge chair in the center of his spacious office inside his cliff side villa located on the west coast of the Greek Island of Naxos, overlooking the Mediterranean Sea and the surrounding islands.

Sitting across the coffee table sat Ara Ceros and Kevin Whitehead.

George Aristotle was an imposing figure. He stood a little over six feet tall and was dressed in a floral short sleeved silk shirt and khaki Bermuda shorts exposing large hairy extremities in contrast to his shaved tanned head.

"We're not sure yet," Ceros said, adding, "We have our best computer people working on it."

Beads of sweat formed on Ceros' wide forehead and he felt uncomfortably over dressed in his European tailored dark blue suit and silk purple tie.

Kevin Whitehead leaned forward and said, "Mr. Aristotle, we don't know how deep this hacker penetrated our organization. We don't even know for sure if he uncovered anything substantial. Rest assured, you are not in jeopardy under any circumstances. We just felt you should be made aware of the breach."

"I still haven't heard how this could happen. We spend top dollar on security. How could some hack get into our files?" Aristotle said, looking at Ceros and then Whitehead.

"Rest assured, sir, we will get to the bottom of this and the people responsible will be dealt with," Whitehead said confidently.

***

Jess introduced his friends to Joe Jimenez as they met and sat down at a corner table inside Bailey's Saloon on Main Street in Douglas, Arizona.

"I'm real sorry to her about your dad," Jesse began. "I remember him as a good man and an asset to our community."

"Thank you Jesse. We buried him this morning," Joe said looking away. Turning back he added, "We're kind a proud of you too. You're a real hero around these parts. What brings you home?

"Joe, what I'm about to tell you cannot go further than this table. Do you understand?"

"Not really, but I think you know you can trust me and if has anything to do with my Dad, like I think it just might, let me hear it," Joe replied.

"I can only tell you that our group believes with good reason, that the people responsible for your father's death go much higher than some drug lord's assassination order. We represent a group of concerned citizens that are determined to get to the bottom of atrocities like what happened to you father and bring them to justice," Jesse said.

Joe thought for a moment and then asked, "How can I help?"

"Is there anyone in local law enforcement you can trust," Chalmers inquired.

"Billy Burnett is the Undersheriff. You might remember him, Jesse. He was in my class in high school," Joe replied without hesitation.

"When can we meet him?" Jesse said.

"Let me call him. He lives just a couple of miles outside of town."

After making the call he said, "Said he'd meet us in half an hour at the substation here in town."

They finished their beer and as they got up to leave Joe looked at Jesse and said, "By the way, Billy is now my boss, I'm a deputy sheriff."

Jesse mumbled, "I should have known," as the group made their way out of the bar, across the street and down a block to the substation. It was a large open room with several desks behind a counter and two holding cells lining the back wall.

Billy Burnett was already there sitting behind a desk in the corner. After introductions were made, Ian said, "I'd like to thank you Undersheriff Burnett, for meeting with us. Let me start by saying we do not represent any government authority and have no official credentials and I say respectfully, you have no obligation to speak to us."

Burnett leaned back in his chair and folded his hands on his ample belly and said. "Well, no disrespect intended, but I don't give a good god damned who you are or where you're from. I've had it up to my ass with those fuck'n suits from Washington Dee Cee. They swooped down here like a bunch of vultures on a coyote carcass and ordered me and my deputies off my own crime scene. That really chaffed my hide, so I'll talk to any god damned son of a bitch I care to. And drop the bull shit and call me Billy."

Grant couldn't stifle a laugh and said, "Man, you Texas boys sure don't pull your punches, do you?"

"If I may ask," Chalmers said, "when you say the Washington D.C. suits took over your crime scene, who in particular were you talking about?"

Burnett told them within an hour after he and his deputies had arrived on the scene at Sheriff Jimenez' home and Marlene Jimenez had been taken to the hospital, a helicopter landed with three FBI agents who took over the crime scene. Burnett and his deputies were ordered off the property and told not to talk to anyone, especially the media."

Ian, without going into detail and withholding names, hypothetically described to Joe and Billy 'Operation Montezuma's revenge'.

When he finished, Billy looked at Joe and said, "That sure beats the hell outta the official version of how Pablo Vasquez met his demise that we got."

Jesse looked at Joe and said, "Our bottom line agenda now is the same as your father had. Right now we're just interested in investigating and finding out who would want to silence him and who did it."

Billy looked at Joe and then to Jesse with a raised eye brow and said, "I think you should meet Maria Hernandez. She's the Chief of Police of Aqua Prieta, the Mexican town that shares its border with Douglas. I'll call her and see if I can get her over here for a meeting in the morning."

***

"Chalmers, its' Mary, the mother fuckers did it. Watson's dead," Dinosa said into her phone.

"Whoa, slow down Mary. What are you talking about?" Chalmers said as he toweled off in the bathroom of his Motel Eight room.

Dinosa sighed and said, "They found Luke Watson dead in his sell this morning. The initial report says there was no sign of foul play. I'm on my way to meet Valerie at the Federal Building. Where the fuck are you?"

Chalmers paused to think for a moment and Dinosa said, "Chuck...Chuck, are you still there?"

"Yeah, just give me a second," Chalmers growled.

Finally he asked, "Where's the body?"

"Christ, I don't know. The prison morgue would be my guess," she replied.

"Find out who's doing the autopsy. If Valerie can swing it, have her insist Doctor Zack Peterson do it. He's the Marin County Coroner. At least collect a blood and stomach content sample. Call Sean Armstrong and let him know what's going on and Dinosa..." he paused.

"Yes?" Dinosa said.

"Keep me posted," Chalmers couldn't help himself.

"Fuck you," Dinosa said.

Chalmers chuckled to himself as he dressed. He had to admit he missed the days the two of them shared while working in Homicide.

He answered a knock at the door and greeted Ian, Grant and Jesse. They piled into their rental SUV and drove northeast out of Douglas. Jesse was driving and pulled off the highway onto a dirt road several miles out of town and crossed a cattle guard.

"Maria Hernandez agreed to meet us, but insisted it be at a remote location. I guess she's pretty paranoid and for good reason. Any police authority in Mexico that doesn't cow tow to the cartels has a short life span. Hell, that's becoming true in this country.

"Anyway, Billy decided this would be a good place to meet. We can detect any unwanted visitors for miles by their dust trail."

The road was bumpy and very dusty as it wound through the dry prairie between patches of wild grass, buck brush and mesquite. They finally came to an ill repaired corral. A Cochise County Sheriff's Bronco was parked looking in their direction as Jesse pulled up. Inside the Bronco were Jimenez, Billy Barnett and a uniformed policewoman.

They were introduced to Maria Hernandez. She was a pretty lady with large brown eyes with grim lines extending away and down. Chalmers guessed her to be in her mid forties.

"So, I finally meet the gringos who decapitated and disemboweled the great 'El Diablo' Pablo Vasquez," she said sarcastically.

"We deny everything," Jesse said smiling and added, "And I take offense to your racist remark lumping me with a bunch of gringos."

He reached out and put a big bear hug around Maria, lifting her off her feet. After letting go of her, she stepped back rearranging her Smokey hat looking a little startled and said, "You're awful forward, ben dejos."

"That I am, Senorita," Jesse roared.

Maria Hernandez was a distant cousin on his father's side that Jesse now recalled meeting at family reunions when he was just a boy. He remembered her as a shy older teenager that the boys chased but never caught. The last time he had seen her was ten years earlier at his father's funeral. Unfortunately, he now realized they had little contact on that occasion and none since.

"What is it I can help you hombres with?" she said, now smiling.

Chalmers spoke up, "Well, to start, do you have any information regarding the assassination of Sheriff Jimenez?"

Maria raised an eyebrow and looked suspiciously at them and then said, "I have no proof, but I'd say the 'El Dorado' cartel had something to do with it.

"I'm not sure how he might be involved, but there's a man that lives south of Aqua Prieta. I've had him under sporadic surveillance for the past year. He has many visitors, mostly cartel members and government officials, never at the same time of course. His name is Paulo Mendoza and he owns a large cattle ranch, but the funny thing is he has no cattle.

"The night before last one of my officers observed three men, he believed to be lieutenants in the 'El Diablo' cartel, turn onto the road to Mendoza's ranchero. The next day their car was found about twenty miles west with no sign of the men.

"I believe Mendoza is some kind of a middle man, but again I have no proof. Even if I did it probably wouldn't do any good."

"Could you give us directions to where Mendoza lives?" Ian asked.

"I could, but I don't need any more grief on my side of the border. I already have enough," she replied.

"We won't bring you any grief, we'd just like to talk to him," Jesse said with a wry smile.

***

Chapter Five

"Mom, we can use this as leverage," Jennifer said as she lugged her suitcase into the kitchen and placed it at the back door.

"What on earth are you talking about?" Colleen said as she peeked outside through the curtains on the back door's window.

"Well, the last time we had to hide out at Matt and Shannon's house, we got Pop to promise a vacation anywhere in the world. What to do think we can get this time?" Jennifer asked.

"You are a devious little imp, aren't you? And as I recall, you pretty much enjoyed the last time, as you ay, we had to hideout at the O'Farrell home," her mother retorted.

"Yes, but we can't let Pop know that," Jennifer said mischievously.

Colleen looked back though the window and said, "Here they are. Come on, grab a bag and let's go."

When they opened the door Matthew was already there and his sister was a few steps behind him.

"Can we give you a hand?" Matt asked, picking up luggage.

Sheila stood at the bottom of the stairs and yelled up, "Hi there, can I help?"

"I think we've got it covered," Colleen yelled back.

After they stowed the luggage in the back of the silver SUV, Matt got behind the wheel and had insured the passenger seat next to him was reserved for Jennifer. They began the hour long trip across the Golden Gate Bridge to the Sausalito Hills.

***

"Joe, I'm gonna tell you one more time, I don't think this is a good idea," Jesse said as they crouched down in the orange tree grove with Chalmers, Ian and Grant. They were all dressed in camo outfits with side arms strapped to their thighs and one hundred yards from the cyclone fence that separated the United States from Mexico. They were about five miles west of Douglas.

"With all due respect, fuck you, Jesse. This is my father's murder we're talking about and it you don't want me along, shoot me," Joe said adamantly.

"Jesse, quit your nagging, god damn it," Ian whispered. "I understand perfectly well why Joe wants in on this."

Jesse sighed and said, "Okay, let's go then."

The group ran in a crouch across the open field until they reached the fence. Joe knew from time spent with the border patrol that this location was a blind spot for the surveillance cameras that monitored the border.

Jesse and Grant removed digging utensils from their back pack holsters and began digging a hole in the sandy loam under the fence. One by one they crawled under and proceeded to run the twenty yards to the top of a shallow arroyo. They descended the bank and walked down the gully until they came to a ditch next to Mexico Highway Two.

They lay down in the ditch and waited. Chalmers looked at his watch which read 2:20 am. There was little traffic on the highway. About ten minutes later a set of headlights approached from the east. The car slowed and blinked its lights off and on twice. The men jumped up and filed into the older model Jeep Cherokee.

As the jeep pulled off the shoulder and onto the highway, Jesse introduced the driver.

"This is Orlando, another cousin," Jesse said.

They drove two miles west and then turned off onto a gravel road heading south. They proceeded down the gravel road for about four miles when Orlando pulled off the road and parked in a small grove of scrub oak trees.

"About fifty meters up this road you will find another road going east. Senor Mendoza's casa is about half a mile up that road around a turn and out of sight. If you climb to the top of the hill where the road turns you will be able to see his casa below. I will wait here for you," Orlando said.

The group piled out of the jeep. The clear starry night provided enough light to see their surroundings. They followed the road that led to Mendoza's hacienda until they came to a turn in the road and the hill Orlando had described. They scaled to the top which overlooked the hacienda and the grounds surrounding it.

They all put on night vision glasses and observed the ranch style single story home that sat just below them. The house was dark except for light that emitted from a covered outside front porch. Fifty yards across the front yard was the ranch hands barracks and on the far side a barn with an attached coral.

"Okay," Ian whispered, "we don't know for sure the number of guards or household help. Jesse, you and Grant secure the barracks. Don't let anyone disturb us. When you're in position you should have visual on the front of the house and porch, Signal me with the number of guards on the porch."

Jesse nodded and he and Grant proceeded slowly down the hill. They circled far from the house and approached the barracks on the far side quietly. Grant took up a position on one side of the barracks and Jesse on the other. They observed only one guard asleep on the porch. Jesse removed an infra red pointer from his shirt pocket and flashed it once in the direction of Ian.

Seeing the flash, Ian turned to the others and said, "You wait here and I'll give you the come on when I've secured the outside of the house."

He silently descended the hill and approached the porch. He could see the guard sitting on a lounge chair breathing softly with his eyes closed on the far side of the porch. His AK47 automatic rifle leaned against the wall next to him.

Ian moved to the far side of the porch and crept up behind him. He removed his combat knife from its sheaf. He reached up and around the man's head and cupped his free hand over his mouth while placing the tip of his eight inch razor sharp blade in the man's nostril, nicking it and drawing a trickle of blood.

The man woke with a jolt, his eyes wide. Ian whispered menacingly in Spanish, "Do as I say and you will live."

The man's body stiffened and he gave a slight nod. Ian moved the blade to the man's throat.

"I'm going to remove my hand and when I do you will remain totally quiet and motionless, comprende?" Ian said.

Again the man nodded. Ian unclasped his hand and removed his revolver from its holster, placing the barrel to the man's temple. He stepped over the railing and onto the porch.

"How many more guards are inside" He whispered.

"There are no more guards inside, I swear, only two senoritas in his bed. I beg you, do not kill me," the man pleaded.

The man told Ian the location of Mendoza's bedroom and repeated, "Please senor, don't kill me."

"I won't kill you," Ian said and pulled a syringe from the thigh pocket of his fatigue trousers. He plunged it into the man's neck while holding him up. Almost instantly the man's eyes rolled up into their sockets and he went limp. Ian laid him gently on the deck.

He walked to the front from under the awning and motioned to his friends to join him.

Chalmers and Joe stood behind Ian as he flipped on the light of Mendoza's bedroom.

"If anybody moves or yells we will kill you," Ian barked out in Spanish.

Mendoza and one of the women bolted upright in the bed. The other girl rolled over and looked up sleepily.

"What the…?" Mendoza started.

"Did you hear me?" Ian said. "Not a word!"

He turned to Chalmers and said, "Would you put the young ladies in another bedroom please?"

Chalmers allowed the two naked women to put on robes and escorted them to an adjoining bedroom where he bound and gagged them. When he returned he found Mendoza sitting bound and naked in a chair with Ian and Joe standing over him.

Ian nodded at Joe who then looked down at Mendoza and said, "Do you know who I am?"

Trembling, Mendoza looked up and sniveled, "No, senor."

"My name is Joe Jimenez. I'm the son of the late Sheriff Edwardo Jimenez..."

Mendoza rolled his eyes wildly and then squeezed them shut. Tears of fright streamed down his cheeks and he whimpered, "I'm sorry, but you must believe I had nothing to do with that. I swear on my mother's grave."

"Who did?" Joe growled.

"It was the 'El Diablo' cartel and I avenged your father's death. I executed those responsible. I can show you pictures of their bodies," Mendoza stammered, sweating profusely.

"Where are the pictures?" Ian demanded.

"Over there in the top drawer of my desk," Mendoza said nodding toward a desk in the far corner of the room.

Chalmers walked over and retrieved a blank envelope from the top drawer of the desk. It contained a stack of photographs. Thumbing through them, he walked back and shared them with Ian and Joe.

The first three pictures were shot from various angles and showed three men lying in a shallow grave somewhere in the desert. The next four photographs were taken from a telephoto lens in rapid succession. The first showed the front of Sheriff Jimenez's home with his wife standing at the open front door waving goodbye to her husband sitting behind the wheel of his patrol vehicle. The next one was just a ball of fire that obliterated and hid the house. The third picture showed the crumpled debris of the vehicles frame with smoke rising and still blurring the view of the home. The last photograph showed the crumpled Bronco's frame, the damaged front of the home with windows shattered and a vacant front door way.

Joe winced and his hands involuntarily covered his face as he turned away.

"These pictures were taken by the same camera," Ian bluffed and continued, "Who owns this camera?"

Mendoza squirmed and his facial expression turned to total surrender and terror.

"The camera is mine, senor," he said, quivering.

"What is your connection with 'Save the World Investments' corporation?" Ian asked.

"Senor, I beg you, if I tell you I'm a dead man," Mendoza whimpered.

"If you don't tell me, you're a dead man," Ian replied.

"I only do what they tell me."

"You only do what who tells you?"

"His name is Mr. Whitehead and I only met him once years ago. Now we just talk on the telephone. He tells me what to do and I do it. I am only a facilitator."

Ian handed his combat knife to Joe and nodded.

Joe took the knife and with Mendoza looking up at him with pleading eyes, Joe swiped the knife across his neck. Blood spurted from the wound and Mendoza toppled to the floor dying.

***

186 D. Patrick Carroll

Chapter Six

"This is really scary stuff," Grub said. "I feel like I'm Mel Gibson in the movie 'Conspiracy Theory'."

He and Snoops were sitting in the parlor outside George Armstrong's office in the Armstrong residence. Besides George Armstrong, Sol Goldsmith and Sean O'Farrell were also present in the room.

"Let me make sure I understand what your research has uncovered," Armstrong said, and continued, "You've traced funds from 'Save the World Investments' not only to government officials in at least seven countries, but to political fund raising groups of both parties in this country. That's blatantly against our election laws. How did they do it?"

"It's complicated to say the least, but when you see million dollar payouts to several big political contributors and political fund raising groups, from individuals to dummy corporations and visa versa and for no legitimate purpose, what other conclusion can you draw?

"Couple that with the fact we can prove that most of these funds were generated from illegal drug and arms sales. I believe we've uncovered a conspiracy on a massive scale. We've uncovered direct payments made to top officials in three of the President's cabinets. Let the facts speak for themselves. Read our report," Grub concluded.

"One question," Sean said and asked, "Can they find you two?"

Grub rubbed his chin and said, "I don't know. They can certainly and probably already know they've been hacked, but whether they can trace it back to me, I'm not sure. I've installed propriety software that I've developed and not shared with anyone else, but I'm not so arrogant that I believe it's one hundred percent impregnable."

"Is there any way they can trace your work back to us?" Goldsmith asked.

"Unless they know we're here right now, that would be very unlikely," Grub replied.

"We need to make you two disappear," Sean said.

***

Ara Ceros and Kevin Whitehead sat in the company lounge at the 'SWI' headquarters office in Athens, Greece. They were alone in the room.

"Kevin, Kevin…what the hell is going on over in North America?" Ceros sighed.

"We don't know who killed Mendoza. He was found dead and naked with his throat slit in his own bedroom. Two whores were tied up in the adjacent bedroom and the only sentry said he was drugged and only remembers one gringo. It was obviously a bloody sloppy security system. The two whores say there were two gringos and a Mexican.

"We don't believe it was the 'El Diablo' cartel. They are totally decimated and most of those that survived are now playing for the 'Mexican Mafia'. We can think of no reason or purpose for Morales to kill him, but you never know about that psycho," Whitehead explained.

"Why is it, Englishman, that whenever you have good news it's always 'I' and when you deliver bad news it's always 'we'?" Ceros asked rhetorically, and then added, "Do you have any good new?"

"Yes, we," and he stressed the word we, "have." We're narrowing our search for the hacker and should know who he is soon."

"I assume you've taken steps to handle that situation," Ceros said.

"Yes, we have," Whitehead said with a wry smile.

"And Kevin, find out who killed our good friend Mendoza."

***

The four man team stood on the tarmac next to their corporate Cessna Citation jet with Joe Jimenez and Billy Burnett.

Joe handed Jesse a zip lock bag containing his father's miniature dash board Saint Christopher statue and the rosary beads his father kept draped over his rear view mirror and said, "Keep these safe, will you?"

"I promise these will be returned to you," Jess replied and hugged him.

"Vios con dios, brother," Joe said.

Once inside the plane, Jesse deposited the baggie in his overnighter, turned to Chalmers and said, "We have a friend who can analyze those articles and hopefully she can trace the explosive residue back to its origin."

***

Ian was back in his father's office on the phone.

"Hey Nancy, how's it going?" he spoke into the phone.

Nancy Cromwell and her husband Steve had moved on after operation 'Montezuma's revenge. They had invested in and became the managing and operating managers of a small ski resort on Mount Lassen in northern California and were now living there.

"Just great, it's beautiful up here. When are you guys going to visit? We're just about ready for the season."

"Don't worry, you'll probably get tired of seeing me once the snow starts. Speaking of visiting, I know you guys are busy and I hate to ask, but the foundation was wondering if you could get away for a couple of weeks. We could sure use you," Ian said wincing.

"Actually, we were just talking about how the repairs are almost complete and we should get away for awhile before the season starts. I'm sure Steve will feel the same way and we'd jump at the opportunity to help you out," she said excitedly.

***

Chalmers sat across from Dinosa at what had become their usual table in the corner of Lefty's Tavern.

"They snatched the body right off the autopsy table, Dinosa said incredulously. "I mean, their own protocol says the bodies of deceased inmates at San Quentin will be transported to the Marin County Coroner for autopsy, and then Action Jackson shows up with a couple of his ass lickers from the FBI with a federal court order and takes custody of the body. They gathered up all the blood samples, the scalpels and tools and anything that might have any trace evidence, or at least that's what that asshole action Jackson thought."

Dinosa's lips curled into a wry smile and she continued, "Doctor Peterson told us when they were prepping old Luke for autopsy his assistant cleaned the body. It was a mess. Vomit covered his upper body and prison garb. While cleaning the body the assistant filled a trash container with sponges and gauze. He replaced the plastic bag and placed the old one in the disposal area.

That moron Jackson collected the clothes and the trash container, but neglected the trash in the disposal area."

"Where was Valerie Kane in all of this?" Chalmers asked and added, "I thought she was the lead prosecutor. Wouldn't she be involved in any court order that affected her case?"

"Oh, Val is livid. They went over her head without her knowledge. Her boss initiated the order and a San Francisco Federal Judge rubber stamped it. Chuck, we got fucked and never even kissed," Dinosa concluded.

"Who's Valerie's boss?" Chalmers asked.

"Oh, she's a real ankle. Her name is Ladasha Thompson and she's a real ladder climber. She's the district's senior prosecutor and word has it she's in line to fill the next open Federal Judgeship."

"So, what are the results of the tests conducted on the clean up material?"

"Strychnine," Dinosa said, "they found a lethal concentration of strychnine in Watson's puke."

***

Nancy giggled as Steve walked out of the Armstrong home onto the deck and said, "Look it's Ringo Starr."

Steve, wearing a black shaggy wig, replied, "Ha ha, and you look like the ass end of a '59 Chevy."

Nancy was donned in peddle pushers, a red polka dot blouse and wore a pair of wide rimmed pointed glasses made popular in the 1950's. Her hair was pulled back in a tight pony tail ala the fifties.

"At a distance, I think they'll pass just fine. They're about the same size and build," Grant said, lying on his back in a patio lounge chair.

"You guys are so brave. Are you sure you want to do this?" Snoops said, standing up and hugging Nancy.

"Of course we are. Life was getting a little boring anyhow," Nancy said.

"Staying in a mountain cabin is right up our alley. And hell, we both drive Jeep Wranglers, it's perfect," Steve added and continued, "I'd trade places with the world's smartest man anytime."

"You aren't being so smart now. You're like lambs being led to the slaughter. I'm on record for being against this lunacy. There must be a better way to handle this," Grub grumbled from his patio chair.

Ian interrupted and said, "Grub, you've been trained in the science of computers and you're the best. Give us some credit. We've been trained for mission just like this one and we're the best."

Grub shrugged acceptance and exchanged car keys with Steve and shaking his hand said, "Sorry, best of luck and God speed."

***

"Damn, Senor Morales, we launder your money and we influence the authorities that allow you to stay in business. We got you out of trouble in that bloody cocaine bust. How could you put a hit on a constable without our authorization?" Whitehead said into his phone, sitting in his Athens office.

Eric Morales had been arrested six months ago in what turned out to be the biggest DEA bust in the agency's history. He was arrested for receiving half a ton of cocaine for distribution. He was released the same day on bail and subsequently the charges were dropped with little objection from the prosecutors office.

"Let me say first, any back country public defender could have gotten me off of that illegal arrest," Morales said and with his ire rising continued defiantly, "And secondly, I don't need authorization for anything I do! If that man and his friends succeed in legalizing drugs, it will ruin both of our businesses."

Whitehead was thinking what an arrogant, short sighted little son of a bitch, but said tactfully, "Mister Morales, you're our man. All we ask is that you consider the long term effect of your actions and consult with us before you do something like this again."

"I am my own man!" Morales roared and slammed the receiver down.

***

Steve and Nancy were driving south on Highway 17 in the Santa Cruz Mountains. They had just passed the road side sign that indicated Scotts Valley was five miles and Santa Cruz sixteen miles ahead.

"We want to make the next right," Nancy said, sitting in the passenger seat observing her hand held GPS device.

Steve turned the Jeep onto Stimson Road. A mile and a half later he turned right onto a dirt road with a single mail box set off to the side. The dirt road ahead disappeared into the pine and cedar trees and wound around in an arc until they came to a small meadow with a log cabin nestled in the tree line.

"It's so beautiful," Nancy said, exiting the car and taking in a deep breath.

They began unloading their luggage and provisions. Upon entering the home Steve whistled and said, "This is marvelous. Grub told me he bought this place from an estate sale about a year ago. It was built by a 'flower power' couple in the mid sixties. They hand hewed and notched the logs from the property. Grub says he's spent all his spare time here upgrading the plumbing and electrical but hasn't disturbed the basic layout. The workmanship is superb."

The front door opened into one large room. An open kitchen and small dining area sat off to the right and stairs on the left led to a loft bedroom. The only addition to the original structure was a bathroom and a laundry room attached to the rear of the home.

After stowing their groceries in an already well stocked refrigerator and food cabinets they hauled their luggage up the stairs. The front of the lofted room opened up to the room below. A canopy bed adorned one side and in the far corner was an ell shaped desk with two computer terminals. Above the desks mounted to the wall were four monitors that Grub had told them were connected to corresponding hidden and motion activated cameras covering the entire perimeter of the home and outside grounds.

"Well, they certainly were security conscious," Steve observed.

"It's amazing," Nancy beamed. "Snoopy told me Grub incorporated what he calls 'smart ware' in the system that can recognize if the moving object is human. It also has a light detector and automatically switches to night vision optics when the sun goes down. When armed, if any of the cameras detects human movement outside it turns on subtle red lights in every room in the house and a vibrating mattress in the bed."

She batted her eyes and cooed, "Oooh Ringo, I wonder if there's a bypass switch for that."

***

"We've not been able to trace the origin of our hacker, but our people believe there are but a handful of computer experts in the world capable of cracking our security protocols. Two or three reside in China and I believe we can cross them off the list. We've narrowed it down to two candidates. Hans Braumm lives in Stockholm and the other is Daniel Tanaka who lives in northern California.

"They're both free lancers. Mr. Braumm seems to be the more political of the two and our primary suspect. He authors a blog and discusses everything from the unrest and terrorist activities in the Middle East to state funded lunches in Swedish schools. He considers himself an investigative reporter," Whitehead said sitting across the desk.

"I suggest we err on the side of caution," Ceros said and added simply, "Eliminate them both."

"As you wish," Whitehead replied and continued, "Senor Morales is becoming a genuine problem, in the words of our American friends, a real cowboy. He refuses to accept our authority and insists on doing things his way. He has already become a liability."

"Have you found a suitable replacement for him and his organization?" Ceros asked.

"Not yet, but we're looking. For continuity sake I think we need to find someone already established within his organization that we can control, someone who is ambitious without blind ambitions."

***

Two days later the following headline appeared above the fold in the London Post;

STOCKHOLM MAN KILLED IN CAR BOMBING

Police Say Slaying of Controversial Blogger

Still Under Investigation

***

Steve rolled over in bed and slung an arm over the sleeping Nancy lying next to him. Suddenly the bed started vibrating. They both awoke simultaneously and sat up.

"What the..." Steve started.

"I think we have a visitor," Nancy said.

They both slipped out of bed and hurried to the monitors. They observed two men crouched and approaching the Jeep Wrangler.

One positioned himself at the rear of the vehicle facing the cabin and holding a rifle at the ready. The other man, armed with a flashlight popped the Jeep's hood and pulled an object from his satchel.

Steve retrieved two semiautomatic pistols from the dresser and returned to the monitors. He handed Nancy one of the guns and chambered a round in his.

They watched as the man toiled for several minutes under the hood until he backed away and carefully closed it. He motioned to the other man and they slinked back into the tree line and disappeared from view.

"Thank you Mister Grub," Steve sighed, looking towards the heavens.

Steve and Nancy returned to bed and snuggled.

"That felt pretty neat. Can't you bypass something and turn it back on?" she purred.

"I ain't fix'n what ain't broke, but I can fix you," Steve said reaching up and squeezing her left nipple.

Nancy woke that morning to overcast skies and a light drizzle outside and the smell of cooking bacon. She got out of bed and slipped on a robe and wandered downstairs to the kitchen.

"Morning honey," Steve said, pouring a cup of coffee and placing it on the dinette table. "Bacon and eggs are almost done."

Nancy tilted her head and inquired, "Aren't you a little concerned about that device under the hood of the Jeep? Don't you think we should tend to that before sitting down to breakfast?"

"Already took care of it, or at least most of it, thanks to Grub. Thought I'd save the fireworks until after you got up."

She shrugged and sat down at the table, but did notice, looking out the front window, that the Jeep had been moved a good one hundred and fifty feet from the house.

As the two ate breakfast, Ian and Grant pulled up in an SUV and parked in the front driveway. Steve met them at the door and invited them inside.

"Good morning guys, come on in," Steve greeted them.

"They certainly didn't waste any time," Ian said, taking a cup of coffee from Nancy.

"Yeah, well I disabled the bomb earlier and moved the Wrangler away from the house. I'd be a shame to damage any of this," Steve said spreading his arms and looking around.

"So, was the bomb wired to the ignition?" Grant asked.

"Yes, and all I have to do is reconnect one alligator clipped wire to the negative battery terminal and it'll be rearmed.

Grub said his homemade remote control starter is good for up to a quarter mile away."

After breakfast and coffee the four busied themselves with cleaning up the house and removing any evidence they were ever there. They gathered the computer and monitors along with the hidden surveillance camera and loaded them in the SUV.

As they were leaving the premises, Ian stopped beside the Jeep and Steve got out and reattached the wire arming the bomb. When he returned he reached in his jacket pocket and produced a plastic pill like bottle and holding it up, said, "I managed to keep a little sample of the explosive."

When they reached Stimson Road Steve hit the start button on the remote. Behind them the Jeep didn't even have time to crank over before it disintegrated in a loud explosion and ball of fire. From the road the SUV occupants observed a black cloud rise above the tree line.

"That should give the neighbors a rude early morning wake up call," Nancy chuckled.

***

PART II

Subversion

"Nixon's attempt to order subversion of various departments was bound to come out in some form."
– Bob Woodard

Chapter Seven

The usual early evening fog was forming off the San Francisco coast and cast a purple glow on the rocky shoreline below Sol Goldsmith's Cliff House Avenue home. Gathered on the backyard deck were the members of the 'Justice Foundation' and members of the operational teams.

"Okay, let's review what has transpired, what this investigation has uncovered and where we go from here," Sean Armstrong said.

He continued, "We've all agreed in order to get the illegal element out of the drug trade we need to legalize drugs and set up a legal means and system for there distribution. George Armstrong, our legal mind in the group would like to address this issue."

George Armstrong stood and walked to the front of the room and began, "As a group we have conducted illegal covert operations. We all know that and we've accepted it as the means justifies the end, but what does that end really mean? What happens when, and if, we succeed in legalizing drugs? What kind of bureaucratic chaos would ensue if suddenly drugs were legalized?"

Armstrong paused to let these questions sink in and then continued, "I put these hypothetical questions to the post graduate law students I teach once a week at the Stanford University. I assigned them as a class project to address and resolve these questions. Their conclusions are amazing."

He walked over to a stack of folders piled on top of the wet bar and handed everyone in the room a copy. Each folder contained over three hundred pages.

"I took the liberty of editing and organizing their findings, but you will find this report to be extremely comprehensive. It begins with legislative action to enact the laws, to the U.S. Justice Department, the Commerce Department, the DEA, the FDA and every other government agency down to state and local police departments that would be involved if the laws were changed.

"They also include the private sector involvement that would be necessary from the pharmaceutical manufactures down to the distribution of product to the consumer and interim measures that should be implemented when the illegal supply is suddenly cut off.

"These young people are the best and the brightest and they obviously took this project on with vigor. I asked them not to moralize or express personal opinions."

He looked at Sean and nodded.

Sean cleared his throat and said, "I've read this report and I'm asking all of you to do the same. We need your input, but personally I accept it to be the course we should adopt.

"George has put together a list of Congressmen and other influential people who are on record for the legalization of drugs. When the time is right we will assemble these people and present our plan.

"That brings us to timing and trust. Thanks to Grub and Snoopy we are close to releasing information that should lead to the indictment of several politicians, government authorities and private citizens in this country. The problem is, who can we trust that will and can use this information? The corruption runs so deep that even well minded innocent people could be coerced into interfering with our mission. And for those we can trust and can do something with this information; how do we protect them?"

George Armstrong interrupted and said, "I've taken it on by myself to invite a man named Ulysses Bowen, a friend and free lance journalist to visit me. He is a man we can trust and writes a syndicated nationally published column. He would jump at this story and I could protect him in the comfort of my home. When we decide the time is right, I'll call him."

Chalmers stopped chewing on the end of his pencil and said, "Most of us know Veronica Kane and her investigator Mary Dinosa and their integrity. Let me meet with them and run it by them and see what they say."

Sean looked at his son Ian and asked, "What kind of a threat do you see from 'SWI' and Eric Morales?"

"The player we have to deal with at 'SWI' is an Englishman named Kevin Whitehead. We don't have any reliable connections in Greece and it's going to be difficult to determine his next move.

"We do know his henchman in Mexico has been eliminated and we believe Eric Morales and the 'Mexican Mafia' have replaced 'El Diablo'. Morales lives in Phoenix and I believe we'll be heading there to keep an eye on him."

Chapter Eight

"How do you two propose to deal with this fucking mess in America?" George Aristotle asked, feigning curiosity.

He sat with Ara Ceros and Kevin Whitehead on the veranda of his cliff villa that could better be described as a fortress built into the cliffs on the west coast of the Greek Island Naxos.

"Eric Morales had vehemently denied any involvement in the assassination of Pablo Vasquez and of course we believe he is lying, but what if he isn't? What if there was a third party involved who has no connection with the 'Mexican Mafia'?"

"Go on," Aristotle said.

"Except for the way Vasquez's body was displayed, the rest of the operation does not fit with Morales' mode of operation. Firstly, it was too clean. I don't believe he has the intelligence to pull this off the way it happened. The place was leveled and the Panamanian's plane was high jacked. Where did it go and why would Morales destroy over half a ton of cocaine?

"We've now learned from locals that a group of mysterious Americans visited Vasquez's hacienda the night of his murder and disappeared right after. We believe this group was responsible for his death and the carnage was meant to get our attention."

"Have we identified this group?" Aristotle asked, now with genuine curiosity.

"No, but I believe they'll identify themselves soon," Whitehead replied.

"And when they do...?"

"I think we should entertain their offer. We know Senor Morales cannot be trusted and must be replaced. These people are obviously intelligent and ambitious and may be the answer to our American mess," Whitehead said.

"We need you to travel to the United States for a hands on assessment. Take what you need and depart as soon as possible," Aristotle ordered.

"As you wish," Whitehead said.

***

"Where the hell did you find those?" Ian asked chuckling.

"Fuck you, O'Farrell," Grant said, glancing at him over the opera style binoculars. "I kind of thought military issue glasses might stand out a little."

He and Ian along with Jesse were sitting at an umbrella covered table on the deck outside of the Southern Dunes Gold Club restaurant overlooking the course's eighteenth green.

Grant looked back through the glasses and said, "They finally made it to the green. I still don't know who that is he's playing with."

"Let me have a look," Ian said reaching for the glasses.

Grant pulled them back and remarked, "Are you sure these aren't too elegant for you?"

Ian grabbed the handle of the glasses and put them to his eyes saying, "Fuck you."

He observed a tall lanky man with a gaunt look and a crooked hawk nose lining up about a thirty foot putt. Standing across the green was Eric Morales.

"Well, he must be someone important for Morales to be playing golf with him. I doubt this is just a social outing," Ian commented.

Jesse snapped a photograph through the telephoto lens of a digital camera just as the man looked up to follow the path of his put.

"Let's get that picture to Grub and see what he can come up with," Ian said.

"Already sent," Jesse said.

"Jesse, wait here. Come on Grant, let's go see if we can get close to these characters," Ian said, getting to his feet.

He and Grant walked across the deck and into the bar and exited through the main entrance and down a wide stair case and into the club's pro shop. As they passed the counter, Ian grabbed a couple of score cards and two pencils from a cup. They exited the pro shop and proceeded to the caddy cart drop off area.

They stood comparing score cards and appeared to be in pleasant conversation when three golf carts pulled up. Morales and Whitehead were in the lead cart. In the second cart were two large men, one Hispanic and the other Anglo. The last cart was occupied by two men dressed in white overalls who were obviously caddies employed by the golf course.

Ian reached in his rear pocket and pulled out his wallet. Pulling out some large bills he said, "I still think we pushed on the twelfth hole."

"Come on man, do I have to count the shots for you. We were both on the green in two and you three putted and I was down in two. You bogied and I pared that hole. Pay up chump," Grant said, laughing.

They over heard Morales say to Whitehead, "Hey Kevin, how about a cold one at the nineteenth hole?"

"It'd be my pleasure. Hey Mac," he said looking at the large Anglo man, "stow the bag in the car and tip the caddy then join us in the bar."

He had an obvious English accent.

Ian called Jesse on his cell phone and said, "He Jesse, Morales and his golf partner are heading your way. Based on his accent we think he's Whitehead. Keep an eye on them and we'll join you shortly."

Morales and Whitehead entered the building followed by the large Hispanic man. Mack grabbed a golf bag and headed down the walk toward the front of the building and a line of Limousines parked at the curb side.

As he approached one of the limos the driver popped the trunk and got out.

"Sorry Pete, I'm afraid the boss is stopping for a pint. Can't tell you when we'll be ready to leave," Mack said in a heavy cockney accent.

"That's okay, I'm getting paid by the hour," the driver replied.

Ian and Grant approached the two men from the rear and Ian said, clearing his throat, "Excuse me sir, but I was wondering if you could settle an argument between my friend here and me?"

Mack sat the golf bag down and turned around looking puzzled.

"He said the man you were just with is Nathaniel Barker, the famous magician. I'm saying he's way too young to be him."

As Ian engaged the man, Grant stumbled and reached down, stealthily attaching a listening device to the golf bag.

"He's not Nathaniel whomever, now bug off," Mack said angrily.

"Ha, ha, that's ten more you owe me," Ian said, turning around with Grant and walking back toward the club house.

When they were out of earshot, Grant said, "Magician?"

Ian shrugged and they both burst out laughing.

They joined Jesse back on the restaurant outside deck and ordered a beer. They had passed Morales and Whitehead sitting at a table inside while walking across the lounge.

Jesse's cell phone rang when their beers arrived.

"Hey Grub, let me guess. It's Kevin Whitehead," he answered

"If you already knew, why did you waste my time?" Grub whined.

"Sorry man, but we just found out ourselves," Jesse said into a disconnected phone.

"You guys finish up your beers. I'm gonna go get the car and I'll meet you out front. We're going to find out where Mister Whitehead is staying," Ian said.

***

Chalmers sat the picnic basket down, unfolded and spread out the king sized bed spread on the lawn next to the Aquatic Park with a view of the San Francisco Bay. He retrieved a bottle of water from the basket and took a sip when he noticed Mary Dinosa and Valerie Kane coming up the walkway below.

He waved and got their attention. He had purposely found an isolated area on top of a knoll and they had to trudge up a slight incline on the grass. Halfway up the hill, Valerie stopped, reaching down and removed her high heels.

Chalmers thought if he wasn't married he'd be all over that. Kane was a petite, pretty woman in her early forties with short blond hair. As she bent down to remove her shoes Chalmers' mind started undressing her. She looked up at him as if she could read his thoughts and he quickly averted his eyes and embarrassingly shook the thought from his head.

As they approached him, Dinosa smiled and said, "Jesus Chalmers, you shouldn't have. How many young maidens have you bedded with this little romantic maneuver?"

They all sat down on the blanket and Chalmers handed them each a bottle of water. He pulled three paper plates from the basket and unwrapped and placed a cracked crab on each of them followed by a hunk of sourdough French bread he tore from a round loaf.

He handed them both a napkin and said, "Bon appetite."

"And he knows French. Those maidens didn't stand a chance," Dinosa cooed.

"Ha, ha," Chalmers groaned and then said, "I thought this would be a good place to meet away from the office."

He went on to tell them the findings of the 'foundation'. He included everything their investigation had turned up including the names of government officials and political campaigns who had accepted pay offs and how they were accomplished. He also related what they knew about 'SWI' and the 'Mexican Mafia' including the names of George Aristotle, Ara Ceros, Kevin Whitehead and Eric Morales.

"My question, or I should say questions of you," Chalmers said looking at Kane, "is what do you plan to do with this information? Who of your superiors can you trust to share this with and then how do you proceed?"

Kane wiped a bead of sweat from her forehead and bit her lower lip. She looked at Mary and then at Chuck and said, "Damn you Dinosa and damn you Chalmers. How did I allow you two to suck me into this like I was a first year law student?"

Then she smiled, tilted her head and continued, "Well, as they say, in for a penny in for a pound.

"Actually Chuck, there is no one in the Justice Department I or we can trust. After the fiasco with Luke Watson, I believe my boss acted by someone higher up pulling her strings. I don't know who that would be, but Mary and I have conducted our investigation privately. I don't think anyone in our department knows that we know Watson was poisoned.

"I have, however, shared this information with a trusted friend. His name is Bernard Rusk. He was one of my law professors and my proctor in law school and a trusted friend. He's now a senior analyst with the CIA and lives in Virginia.

"He has agreed to keep our findings secret and will do nothing without consulting me first. He's flying out tomorrow and we're supposed to meet. He says he has some ideas about how we should proceed. I think you should meet him."

"Let me think about that. In the meantime, you guys have to be careful. When the shit hits the fan I strongly suggest both of you take up residence at the O'Farrell estate. I'll let Mary tell you about it," Chalmers said looking at Dinosa.

"I'll think about that," Valerie said.

***

They followed the limo carrying Whitehead north onto Highway 101 past Phoenix into Glendale and took the East Camelback exit to the Phoenician Resort. Jesse was driving their rental SUV and stayed back as the limo turned into the hotel's courtyard. They watched as the limo pulled up to the entrance and a bellhop hurried out to open the rear door. Mack and then Whitehead exited the vehicle and the bellhop retrieved the golf bag from the trunk and followed the two men into the hotel.

Jesse then pulled up behind the limo and Ian said, "Wait here and I'll be right back."

As he entered the hotel lobby he noticed Whitehead and Mack, now holding the golf bag, waiting in front of the elevators along with several other guests. He walked over and stood behind them and then followed them into the lift when it arrived.

Mack swiped a key card through the scanner next to 'The Pharaoh Suite' that was located above the buttons labeled Lobby through Floor 4 on the control panel. Ian pressed the button for the second floor and stepped back.

He exited on the second floor and scampered back down to the lobby where he retrieved a hotel brochure from the information kiosk. He thumbed through the brochure until he came to a map of the hotel layout. He saw that the Pharaoh Suite was located above the fourth floor and was the only room on the fifth floor. He identified the two suites that were located directly beneath it on the fourth floor and walked to the registration counter.

"Do you have reservations, sir?" the young man behind the counter asked.

"No, sorry, this is sort of a spur of the moment thing. A couple of associates and friends of mine were in town for a business conference and decided we'd stay over a couple of days and play some of your wonderful courses. We were hoping you had a suite available," Ian lied.

"I think we can accommodate you, sir. Do you have any preferences?"

"I picked up this brochure and I thought it'd be nice to have one of these two," Ian said, pointing to the two fourth floor suites on the map.

"Let me check," the clerk said and after punching some keys on his terminal he continued, "Wow, you're in luck. The 'Sphinx Suite' is available for the next two nights."

"Perfect, we'll take it," Ian said handing him a credit card.

The clerk took the card and after processing it handed Ian three pass key cards and asked, "Would you like me to page a bellhop, sir?"

"That won't be necessary, thank you. Our luggage is at the Embassy Suites and we'll collect it later."

Ian hustled back out to the SUV and found a security guard in conversation with Jesse.

"Ah, here he is now," he heard Jesse say as he approached the vehicle.

"We're all checked in. Jesse will you park the car and join us in the suite. We're in room 408," Ian said handing him a key card.

"Enjoy your stay," the guard said politely walking away.

Grant was hunched over the transceiver he had set up on a table in the suite's sitting room when Jesse entered the room.

"Let's just hope the golf bag is situated in a strategic location and we're within range. Here we go," Grant said as he depressed the speaker button on the transceiver.

The speaker crackled and then they heard clearly, "Aah, thank you Mack. A good blended scotch is so much nicer on the palate that god awful Mexican beer we had to endure earlier."

"You're welcome Mr. Whitehead. If I may ask, why did you let that bloke beat you? That hack couldn't hit a golf ball straight if his life depended on it."

"Oh Mack, you have to understand the art of tact. You keep your enemy happy until after you've cut his throat. Now, if you don't mind taking your drink out to the lanai, I have a phone call to make. Go check out the bikinis by the pool and enjoy yourself."

There was a pause and then the sound of a sliding glass door opening and closing. A moment later the interluders heard, "Hello, Ara?...I'm fine, thank you. I played a round of golf with our pigeon this morning. God, he's such an arrogant boor... No, he has no idea of his fate...No they haven't, but I think they're close. I noticed two gentlemen outside the club house this morning and several minutes later the same two in the lounge and then one of them followed us into the lift at the hotel several hours later. That's too much to be a coincidence. If I'm correct, the man responsible for killing Pablo Mendoza will soon introduce himself...Ah Ara, not to worry, I always take care of myself, but we do need to at least listen to his proposal... Okay and cheerio."

"Well, so much for our stealth surveillance," Ian winced and continued, "It didn't sound like they know who we are and that's a good thing. It seems they believe we're trying to position ourselves to take over for Eric Morales. Huh, I think we may be able to use this to our advantage."

***

That evening, Ian, and Grant were at the PhoenixDeer Valley Municipal Airport to greet Chalmers and John Garcia as they deplaned from the company jet. The group piled into the SUV for the twenty minute ride back to the Phoenician Hotel.

"So, how do we approach this Mister Whitehead?" Ian asked.

"John and I discussed on the plane the recent developments and, if it's true they believe our group was responsible for killing Mendoza and our intentions are to take over his business, we have to present ourselves in the most honest light possible. Our personal lives will be vetted and if they suspect any of our information is a lie or we are trying to entrap them, the results could be disastrous," Chalmers said and continued.

"John will present himself as a former DEA agent gone rogue after discovering the betrayal of he and his family by the agency. He met me during the investigation of the Barnes family massacre, which I took personal interest in.

"I will present myself as a retired SFPD homicide inspector and the two of us partnered up to avenge his betrayal and my personal loss. During our investigation we discovered the 'El Diablo' SWI connection and hired the late Doctor Tanaka to gather intel on their operation.

"The team we assembled to go after Pablo Mendoza fit perfectly into our new plan to take over the transportation and distribution of illegal drugs into the States.

"Since you and Grant are already known to them, you'll have to make the introductions. From there we'll have to play it by ear. We already have enough evidence to indict Whitehead, Ceros and Aristotle but we're a long way from bringing them and other guilty parties to justice."

Ian's cell phone rang and interrupted their conversation. He answered, "Hey, Jesse, what's up?"

"After supper I followed them to the Cairo Lounge. It's located just off the lobby. He and Mack are having an after dinner drink and it appears Whitehead is quite the lady's man. He's yucking it up with what I believe to be a lady of the night," Jesse replied.

"Stay there and we'll meet you in about ten minutes," Ian said.

***

Valerie Kane and Mary Dinosa pulled into the courtyard of the San Francisco Mark Hopkins Hotel that sat atop Nob Hill. Kane was excited about seeing her old professor and mentor whom she hadn't see for years. She remembered him as a very resolute and dedicated instructor who stressed the importance of professional and personal ethics. The other law students called him 'Saint Bernard' and when a student from Uruguay tagged him 'Los Santos', it stuck.

In the passenger seat Dinosa turned to Valerie and said, "Wow, you know I've lived in the city all my life and I've never been here."

"Me either," Kane said, "never thought I could afford it."

A man in a Falstaff uniform opened Dinosa's door and a valet parker opened Kane's door. Exiting, she handed him the keys.

The Falstaff man asked Dinosa, "Any luggage, Mum?"

"Ah...No thank you, we're just guests," she replied a little flustered.

He escorted the two women to the grand entrance and opened the door. Dinosa didn't know if it was appropriate to tip him or not and concluded it'd be less embarrassing not to than offer one and have him ignore her.

They found the elevators and Dinosa said, "Mum? Do I look that old?"

They were both giggling nervously as the elevator arrived and they stepped into the lift. Kane pressed the button identified as 'Top of the Mark'.

The elevator opened into a large foyer with a coat room on one side and the entrance to the restaurant and lounge on the far side. They walked to the desk and met an Amazon, very pretty blond woman dressed in a black full length low cut gown.

Dinosa thought a small person could get lost in her cleavage.

"Mr. Rusk, please" Kane said.

"Oh, Mr. Rusk is waiting for you in the lounge," she cooed and motioned for an usher.

As they followed the usher around the dining room and into the lounge, Dinosa nudged Kane and said in a low voice, "Jesus Christ, that woman had enough plastic in her lungs she wouldn't need a life jacket if she fell overboard in heavy seas."

Valerie chuckled on the verge of hysterical laughter and managed to say, "Hush."

Bernard Rusk was sitting at the far end of the bar when they found him. He stood when they approached and said, "Valerie, you look gorgeous. If I were a younger man, you'd be in a heap of trouble."

After hugging, Kane introduced Mary Dinosa and they took stools at the bar.

"This place in renown for making one hundred and one martinis, should I get you a menu?" he asked.

"No thanks. I'll have a number one hundred and Mary will have a number one hundred and one," Kane said, looking at Dinosa for approval.

After Dinosa nodded, Rusk said, "You always were the adventurous sort."

They sipped on their martinis and talked about old times. When the glasses were empty, Rusk said, "Well, we have a lot to discuss. Why don't we retire to my suite and get comfortable?"

As they waited for the elevator Rusk commented, "My god, if that hostess had any bigger balloons, they'd have to anchor her down. She'd put Carol Dodda to shame."

Kane and Dinosa now burst out laughing.

Once inside Rusk's suite they all sat around a coffee table in the sitting room. In the light, Kane noticed the change in Bernard's appearance. Of course he looked older that she remembered twenty some years ago when he was a vibrant Harvard Law Professor, but somehow he appeared sadder.

Maybe, she thought, it was the years with the CIA and the ugliness he had seen.

Suddenly he perked up and said, "This shit you've gathered is going do more than just upset the apple tree, it's going to shake the whole fucking forest."

Dinosa thought, I'm going to like this guy.

"I've reviewed the material you provided me and except for a few tees to cross and eyes to dot, you've got the evidence to back it up.

"I have to ask you a question. This group of people you call your friends but won't identify that helped you gather this information and evidence, I assume have no legal standing. Do I assume correctly?"

"Yes you do and that's my dilemma. If I can't trust my boss or even her boss and I can't trust the judges, how do I present this? What do I do with this shit, as you call it? That's why I asked for your assistance."

Rusk thought for a moment and then said, "I appreciate your position and let me say I'm honored that you put your trust in me. Obviously, you can't go to your boss with this and any public airing would give the opposition a heads up and jeopardize the entire operation. Everything must be coordinated to happen simultaneously and it must happen soon.

"Let me sleep on it and let's meet again tomorrow morning. There's a great little café just a block down the hill on the corner of Powell Street. How about we meet at nine for breakfast?"

***

The five JF members strolled into the Cairo lounge. Chalmers, Garcia and Ian took a booth along the near wall while Grant sat down next to Jesse at a nearby table. They all noticed Whitehead and Mack sitting in a booth on the opposite wall with two young women dressed in slinky evening gowns.

"Did you notice who just walked in?" Mack said, nodding his head toward the booth of the new arrivals.

Whitehead took his eyes off the ample cleavage of the blond at his side and glanced in the direction of Mack's nod. He removed his hand from her thigh and mused, "Hmm, sooner that I thought."

After their drinks were ordered and delivered, Ian got up and walked across the room towards the Whitehead party.

As he approached their booth, Mack reached under his coat with his right hand.

"Whoa, cowboy, this is a friendly visit," Ian said.

After a nod from Whitehead, Mack removed his hand and laid it on the table.

"Mr. Whitehead, you probably recognize me from our chance encounters this morning. My name is Ian O'Farrell," he said, extending his hand.

"As a matter of fact, I do recall seeing you on several occasions this morning, only I don't believe they were chance encounters," Whitehead said, shaking Ian's hand.

"You're very astute, Mr. Whitehead, but this probably isn't the appropriate time to discuss business. My associates and I are, however, very anxious to arrange a meeting at your earliest convenience," Ian said.

"May I ask, what business it is you'd like to discuss?"

"We have a proposal to offer you after the demise Senor Eric Morales," Ian said seriously, looking at Whitehead through squinted eyes.

"How about a late breakfast meeting in the morning," he said, glancing at his date. "Say around ten o'clock in my suite. I'm staying here in the…"

"Pharaoh Suite, we know," Ian interrupted. "See you sharply at ten a.m. then, cheerio."

***

"Good morning ladies," Bernard said, rising to greet Dinosa and Kane.

He was sitting at a table in the sidewalk dining area outside of the café.

After the women sat down and pleasantries made, Bernard said, "After considering your dilemma, I've come to several conclusions and the first one is, you were wise to consult me."

He feigned a look of superiority and continued, "If there's one thing I've learned from my years at the Capitol, it's you must fight fire with fire, blackmail with blackmail. What you've uncovered, and I can tell you we at the CIA have known part of it for some time, does reveal, dare I say, a vast government and political conspiracy.

"I must warn you that to air this publicly now would result in catastrophe. Yes, it probably would stimulate some kind of a congressional inquiry that would take years to resolve. In the end it would probably force several government officials and politicians to resign and maybe even a few criminal indictments, but it would also put the lives of innocent people in jeopardy.

"Allow me to carry the political ball. I have the connections high up in the Federal Judiciary and I know whose buttons to push. You tell me when the time is right and I'll make sure you get your indictments. When that happens, I suggest you two find a good safe place outside of your office to conduct your business."

Kane raised an eyebrow and asked, "And just how are you going to accomplish that?"

Bernard shrugged and answered, "With fire and blackmail."

"Uhuh, Professor, you have to be more specific that that," Dinosa said sternly.

Rusk took a bite of his eggs benedict and a sip of coffee.

"I guess it won't hurt to tell. I know the Solicitor General, Emory Hancock. In fact, I've submitted reports to his office and have been interrogated in closed sessions by he and his people on matters of national security that have been uncovered by my agency.

"He is, of course, close to the President and he's an arrogant son of a bitch, but he knows I know how his office has spun the truth and at times have buried the truth in matters that the American people should know.

"After we meet, he'll realize the first domino is about to fall and he'll do whatever it takes to distance himself from the domino in front of him and the White House."

"You know this will destroy your career and possibly put your life in jeopardy," Kane said.

"Career, are you kidding me?! They should have put me out to pasture years ago. Oh, and they wouldn't hesitate to put a bullet between my eyes if they thought for an instant that would solve their problems. It's too late for that. No, killing me would serve no purpose and they realize that would be adding fuel to the fire. I don't think my life will be in jeopardy.

"By the way, why do I get the idea your 'friends' have a different or higher agenda in all of this?"

Kane looked up and then back at Rusk and said, "They do. For obvious reasons I can't divulge their identities, but simply put, they believe our government should legalize drugs. I'm not sure if I sympathize with their position or not. At this time, I am only interested in bringing these bastards to justice. They believe revealing the corruption within our own government and putting it in proper prospection will build public support and help their cause."

"I had a strange feeling that was the case," he said, pulling a brown envelope from this briefcase and handing it to Kent.

"This is a report compiled by my department. Please see that it gets in the proper hands. It contains official numbers and statistics compiled by my department as they apply to our war on drugs, which, by the way, I believe we are losing. I'm sure this material will help in their efforts. Feel free to review it yourselves. It may prove helpful as you build your case."

Valerie grabbed hold of Rusk's aging, wrinkled hand and asked, "Bernard, are you sure you want to get that involved in this?"

"Hell, I'd strip naked in front of the Pope to be part of this," he answered with a broad grin.

Dinosa's mouth fell open and before she could say anything, he winked at her and said, "Vee have friends everywhere."

***

Garcia, Ian and Chalmers were met by Whitehead and Mack as they stepped out of the elevator and into the foyer of Whitehead's suite.

Mack frisked the three men and Whitehead said apologetically, "Sorry, gentlemen, but a man in my position can't take any chances."

Chalmers remembered Pablo Ramirez had said something very similar the night he died.

"Perfectly understandable," Ian replied.

"Please come in and partake of a wonderful breakfast. Mexican beer is dreadful, but I must say their cuisine is bloody delightful," Whitehead beamed.

The room was set up with a buffet style table. They each gathered a plate and piled them high with huevos rancheros and other Mexican delicacies before sitting down at a table on wheels.

Ian noticed the gold bag was situated perfectly in a corner of the room.

The discussion started by Whitehead saying, "Mr. O'Farrell, I gathered from our brief conversation last evening that you gentlemen have a proposal to offer me, but first thing first. Tell me something about yourselves."

Garcia took the lead and told Whitehead their rehearsed story including details of operation 'Montezuma's Revenge'. He concluded by saying, "We've done our homework and we know how 'Save the World Investments' is involved in laundering the money and your dealing with the political influencing. We are perfectly willing to accept that relationship and your leadership."

"We've known about your group for sometime, although we didn't identify you specifically as the players. With all due respect, allow me to do a little homework," Whitehead said, picking up the phone and dialing a number.

He related to the person on the other end the names and specifics he'd just been given and ended by saying, "Please, get back to me with due haste."

"Now," he said, hanging up the phone, "please continue."

Chalmers said, "We believe you are unhappy with your present arrangement with the 'Mexican Mafia' and specifically Eric Morales and the purpose of your trip here is to resolve that problem. We also believe you would welcome the chance to not only eliminate an arrogant and foolish partner, but replace him with someone who is willing and able to take his place."

"If I'm hearing you correctly, you're saying you would kill Senor Morales. What do you have in place to take over the distribution and what's to say we wouldn't have the same problems with you?" Whitehead asked.

"Firstly," Ian said, "We haven't moved on Morales until now because we wanted your permission. That should tell you something about our intentions and spirit of cooperation. To answer your first question I can tell you about our plans for taking over the distribution.

"I am the benefactor of our group and I'm sure your research will tell you I have considerable assets. I now want a return on my investment. I also have some well trained men on our team whom you'll also discover are ruthless.

"We are positioned to not only take out Morales but also all of his top lieutenants simultaneously, when we receive your permission, of course. You may have noticed the Mexican gentleman in our group last night. His name is Jesse Leone and soon to be the president of a biker gang called 'Los Banditos'.

"You probably know they are the distribution and enforcement arm of the 'Mexican Mafia'. These are a violent and ruthless group and only fear and respect anyone who is more violent. We will be in a position to control them."

"Well, I must say your proposal has perked my interest and we will seriously consider it. Give me a day or so and please don't implement the rest of your plan until we meet again."

***

PART III

The Solution

*"The only difference between a problem and a
solution is that people understand the solution."*
—Charles F. Kettering
(A quote my father would have appreciated.)

Chapter Nine

"Bernard, it's time," Valerie Kane said into her phone. "We're ready to go forward with Rico charges, but I need the indictments sealed, and I have another problem. As you know, the list is long and these people are located all over the country. How do we simultaneously serve them when the time comes?"

"I'll get you your sealed indictments and if you give me a twenty four hour heads up, I'll also take care of serving the warrants. From the information you provided, I've compiled a list of the defendants. Let's compare lists to assure no one slips through the cracks," Rusk replied.

After comparing notes, Kane had several names to add. Among them were a corrections officer at San Quentin, a customs official at the Port of San Diego, her boss, Ladasha Thompson and FBI Special Agent Jack Jackson.

"I must tell you, some of these people you've added will be tough to prosecute. We have no proof that they actually broke the law. They can claim they were only following orders from their superiors," Rusk said.

"That may be true, but it will certainly shake them up and we'll need their testimony to collaborate other evidence and witnesses we've gathered. We also need to send a message to everyone that is entrusted with public service. Six million Jews were slaughtered because people were just following the orders of their superiors."

"Valerie, spoken like the fiery young law student I remember," Bernard chuckled.

"Whew," Valerie said after hanging up and looking across the desk at Sean O'Farrell and then glancing at Mary Dinosa. "We're committed now."

"Our team in Arizona said they should clean things up there tonight and George Armstrong says his media blitz is ready and awaiting word from you," Sean said.

Valerie crossed herself, looked toward the heavens and sighed, "I guess tomorrow is DDay."

"That'll be good timing for us. We can break the story on Friday and it'll make all the weekend news shows," Sean said.

"Come on, Kane. You need a break. Let's go down to the gym for a work out. You won't believe the facility Mr. O'Farrell has here," Dinosa said, standing up and grabbing Kane's elbow.

***

Ian, Grant and Jesse parked their dirt motorcycles and walked the few yards to the top of the crest to their west. They crouched and peered down at the ranch style home of Eric Morales three hundred yards away.

Grant and Jesse opened the cases they were carrying and assembled the sniper rifles with attached high powered scopes and bipod supports. They all assumed prone positions.

The home sat alone at the end of a paved road that connected to a main artery a half mile down the valley that led to the Phoenix area. They watched as a black SUV backed out of an adjacent garage and pulled around to the front of the house and parked in the circular driveway.

Ian peered through a pair of high powered binoculars and said, "Get ready, guys."

The door to the home opened and two men emerged and proceeded down the walk toward the SUV.

"Jesse, your target's on the left and Grant, you got the right," Ian said.

The men were about halfway to the vehicle when Ian said, "On the count of three, two one."

The two shots rang out in unison. Through the binoculars an instant later, Ian saw the heads of both men explode and disappear in a spray of red as they crumpled to the ground.

Grant and Jesse disassembled their weapons and put them back in their cases. Ian picked up the two spent shells and they hurried back to their motorcycles for the trip back to the Phoenician Hotel.

They returned the rented motorcycles and walked to their suite.

Chalmers was sitting in an arm chair sipping on a beer as the three entered.

"Mission accomplished," Ian said. "What have you learned?"

Chalmers turned down the hissing volume on the transceiver on the table next to him and said, "Oh, I just got off the phone with Mr. Whitehead. He already received the news of Senor Morales' and his top lieutenant's deaths and is quite impressed with the quick and efficient operation after he gave us the okay. He wants another meeting this evening."

"Good, I'll call the old man and let him know it's a go on our end," Ian said.

***

"Goddammit Kane," Dinosa moaned, "If I hear you toss and turn one more time, I'm gonna come over there and ram my size eight double E right up your..."

"Jesus Mary, are your feet that big?" Valerie chuckled.

Dinosa returned the giggle and said, "Yeah, you oughta see the shoe salesman when he tries to fit these clodhoppers."

The two women had become room mates in a second story bedroom in the O'Farrell home when they became convinced their lives would be in danger after their operation became public. Neither of them liked the arrangement, but they reluctantly accepted it.

"Mary, can I ask you a personal question?"

"You just did," Dinosa said, paused and added with an exaggerated sigh, "Yeah, go ahead."

"Why did you become a cop? I mean, you're father is a city councilman and your parents are rich. You could have done and been just about anything you wanted, why a cop?"

"Hmm, I guess it started out with my youthful rebellious attitude. My parents, especially my father was totally against it, and that only made me more determined. After I got into it, I found I really liked it. It was something about catching the bad guy that turned me on. There's no politics involved when you're slapping the cuffs on some perverted scumbag."

Valerie smiled to herself and said, "Have you ever questioned where to draw the line? I mean, when is it justifiable to break the law in order to protect the law?"

"Yeah, especially since I got involved with that fucking Chalmers and this group," Dinosa answered and continued, "I'm not going to go into detail, but when we went after Pablo Vasquez, we broke about half the laws of this country and several international ones and I had a hard time reconciling my involvement.

"Obviously I did, or I wouldn't be here now."

"How?" Valerie asked simply.

"Chalmers put it pretty simple. He says 'good' is the absence of 'evil', and since there will always be evil it's essential that we minimize or at least try to neutralize it with doing 'good'. We all have to come to terms with our definition of the two words," Dinosa explained.

"Thank you for that," Valerie said. "Hopefully, tomorrow will tell how much good we've accomplished."

"Great, now can we go to sleep? I have an early morning flight to catch and I get to take my cuffs."

***

Chapter Ten

Valerie Kane walked into Ladasha Thompson's office, flanked by two U.S. Marshals. Thompson looked up from behind her desk and looking confused demanded, "What's going on here?"

"Ms. Thompson, please stand up, turn around and place your hands behind your back. I'm placing you under arrest. I have a federal arrest warrant charging you with conspiracy to murder, conspiracy to engage in illegal activities in an ongoing illegal enterprise and illegal abuse of your office covered under several federal statutes.

"You can read the warrant later in your holding cell. Now, you have the right to remain silent. You have the right..."

"You have no authority to do this," Thompson spat out, "I'm your boss for Christ sake!"

The two Marshals stepped forward and one grabbed Thompson by her arm and tuned her around.

"You mother fucking bitch! You cunt, I'll see you hanged in a public square! You ungrateful daughter of a bitch!" she yelled over her shoulder at Kane, drool oozing down the corners of her mouth.

Kent looked at the Marshals and said, "That's a new one. I've never been call a daughter of a bitch."

***

Seven hundred miles away, Chalmers stood on the eighteenth green at the Camelback North golf course watching Whitehead line up a twenty foot putt.

Mack approached his boss and said, "Excuse me Mr. Whitehead, but I think you should take this."

He held out a cell phone. Whitehead gave him an angry look and took the phone.

"Hello, who is this?"

As he listened, his angry look turned to confused and then his face lost all color and he dropped the phone to his side and looked around.

He saw a woman and a large man coming toward him from the walkway leading to the green with their firearms drawn. Standing beside him, Mack reached for his pistol under his sweater at the small of his back.

"Sir, that would be a very bad idea," came a voice from behind him as two men stepped out from behind a hedge row that guarded the opposite side of the green. Their pistols were trained on the two Englishmen.

"Mr. Whitehead, my name is Mary Dinosa, Special Agent with the U.S. Justice Department, and I'm placing you under arrest. Please turn around."

"You can't do this," Whitehead protested. "I demand to see the British Ambassador, now!"

"Yeah, and I want to sleep with Pierce Brosnan," Dinosa said, slapping the cuffs on Whitehead and winking at Chalmers.

***

Later that evening more daily newspapers across the nation published special extra editions since September 11, 2001. The headline in the San Francisco Transcript read:

OVER 60 GOVERNMENT AND POLITICAL OFFICIALS INDICTED IN GIANT STING OPERATION
Justice Department Says More Arrests Pending

Under the byline of Ulysses Bowen the story began;

The U.S. Justice Department, throughout today, has arrested more than sixty people as a result of an unprecedented and ongoing investigation into a vast conspiracy of corruption by top government officials, political campaign leaders and private corporation officers.

Valerie Kane, lead U.S. Prosecutor in the investigation, said, "I can only say the arrests of these people are a result of an exhaustive and thorough investigation conducted by the U.S. Justice Department with the cooperation of the U.S. Marshall's Service. Without compromising the ongoing investigation, I can only add that more arrests are anticipated."

This correspondent has uncovered many of the facts surrounding this investigation from sources that have demanded anonymity, but their facts have been independently confirmed. This information, when provided to Prosecutor Kane, opened the investigation led by her office.

The article went on and covered two full pages of the newspaper. It described how the unnamed source had uncovered the connection of major drug cartels to 'Save the World Investments' and payoffs to government officials and political campaigns.

It also listed the names of all those arrested along with the charges against them. The names included the Deputy Attorney General and several of his underlings, the Deputy Director of the DEA, an Assistant Deputy Director and two field office supervising agents of the FBI, three senior officials with U.S. Customs and Immigration, several political campaign chief of staffs and some corporate officers including Kevin Whitehouse.

Bowen also wrote that The U.S. Justice Department had shared information with Interpol and several foreign police agencies, indicating the information provided would lead to investigations and arrests abroad.

A quote from his anonymous source said, "We believe this conspiracy and the corruption that has evolved goes beyond our so called 'war on drugs'. In order to keep their illegal cash flowing, they know perfectly well their activities have to remain illegal. They have now turned their efforts to eliminating the threat from those who would legalize their product. As a result, Arizona, Cochise County Sheriff Edwardo Jimenez and others have paid the prices with their lives. Our 'war on drug' is a complete and utter failure and we must look at other alternatives. Look at where it has led us. Many of our leaders are now the enemy in this war."

***

That night and throughout the weekend the story dominated all the news talk television and radio shows. There was speculation that the investigation would lead to presidential cabinet members and some even brought up the name of the President himself.

Both houses of congress called emergency sessions and initiated their own investigations. The House of Representatives named a special private prosecutor to look into any other official's involvement or corruption.

The midnight oil burned in virtually all of the elected representative's and senator's offices. Elected officials that were out of town cancelled their plans and scurried back to Washington, D.C.

The entire team with their immediate families and Mary Dinosa and Valerie Kane were gathered in the theater room of the O'Farrell Mansion that Sunday evening. The champagne and drinks were flowing along with congratulatory remarks and celebration.

Sean O'Farrell started tapping a spoon on his glass and the noise in the room subsided, "I'd like to announce that, thanks to the hard work of George Armstrong and his law class at Stanford, we have put the final touches on what we're calling the 'National Narcotics Reform' Act. We've presented it to Arizona, U.S. Congresswoman Evelyn Richards and Indiana Senator Lenny Wright who have agreed to coauthor it and present it to their respective houses."

After the applause subsided, Sean continued, "And, it is with great pride and maybe a little prejudice, that I announce John Garcia is throwing his hat into the political ring and will be the next elected U.S. Representative from his native great state of Oklahoma!"

The room erupted into applause and whistles as a make shift air shaft overhead opened and blew red, white and blue confetti over the revelers.

Yells of, "Speech, Speech," echoed in the room.

Garcia rose from his seat, wiping confetti from his hair and shoulders and began, "I'd like to thank each and every one of you for your support. Boy, what a journey. I don't believe we should forget those who started us on this road, so for those of you who'd like to take a knee, I offer the following prayer.

"Lord, we ask for your guidance and for your will to be done. We ask that you relay this message to the Barnes family that we know are by your side. John and Clara and your children Tracy and Randy, we'd like you to know that your lives were not taken from us in vein and that you have been our inspiration and our strength. We know our journey is not over and we have a long way to go, but know you started us on this path and you'll be with us along the way. We know you are now in the safe hands of your Lord and we pray that one day we will celebrate our lives together.

Thank you and thank you Lord. Amen."

THE END

Epilogue

"You know, Ara, this seems like a good time to get out of the drug business and go back to the good old days. No more trading arms for dope. No more dealing with these blood thirsty, idiotic Latinos or the fanatically religious Taliban or anybody else who can't pay cash for our munitions and no more of this money laundering either. I was a fool to get sucked into this from the start," George Aristotle said, sitting in a patio lounge chair across from Ara Ceros on the outdoor terrace of his cliff side villa overlooking the Mediterranean Ocean.

"What about Kevin Whitehead? In the hands of American authorities he knows enough to do serious damage," Ceros asked.

"Fuck that bloody Englishman. It was his genius idea that got us into this mess. No, he can't harm us. The corruption in America goes so high that they will deal with Whitehead just like they did that idiot DEA agent," Aristotle blustered.

Ten miles away at an elevation of ten thousand feet an unmanned drone approached the villa from the northwest. In a bunker buried deep under the Utah Rocky Mountains halfway around the world a young airman sat at a consol controlling the drone's flight.

Peering at the monitor in front of him, he said into his headset, "Target located and tagged."

In a room at the CIA headquarters building in Langley, Virginia, three men stood in front of monitors looking at the same view as the young airman. They saw Aristotle and Ceros lounging on the terrace, a superimposed plus mark over Aristotle's wide chest. Two of the men in the room were dressed in Air Force military uniforms that indicated one was a three star general and the other a full bird colonel. The third man was Bernard Rusk who nodded at the other two.

The colonel said, "Arm weapons system and launch when ready, confirm."

The reply came, "Roger, weapons system armed confirmed, launch when ready confirmed."

"You worry too much my dear friend," Aristotle said, raising his glass in a toast.

That was the last thing he would ever say and the last thing he would ever feel was an intense burning pain as his body disappeared into a mass inferno.

***

The fortress home was built in the sixth century to ward off invading Moors from the south during the Crusades. It sat at the eastern most point of Ile SainteMarguerite off the

French coast a few miles south of Cannes.

Joseph O'Farrell III, Sean's father, had purchased the villa shortly after the end of World War II. He had fallen in love with it's' location and the beauty of the limestone walls and marbled floors. It had been the headquarters for he and his men as the first line of alert and defense from a potential Nazi counterattack in southern France after DDay.

Sheila LamontO'Farrell, Colleen and Chuck Chalmers sat on the top floor deck enjoying the view and sipping wine.

"We used to come here with the family on holiday. The whole famdamily, my parents and grandparents, aunts and uncles and our cousins would congregate here right after Christmas for years. As children we hated the isolation, but as we grew older and were allowed to venture off to the mainland on the ferry, we loved it."

"Speaking of wandering off to the mainland, do you think the children are having a good time?" Colleen asked.

"Well, judging by the way Matthew looks at your daughter, I'd say he'd be happy anywhere in the world," Sheila smiled.

"This was our little blackmailer's idea of anywhere in the world," Chalmers chuckled.

***

Mary Dinosa opened her eyes and looked at the large snowflakes drifting down outside the window. She rolled over and pulled the comforter up higher around her neck and said, "That was so nice of Nancy and Steve to invite us up here."

Ian rolled over and threw his arm around her.

"Excuse me, but I remember you inviting me after they invited you," he yawned.

"You're such an asshole," she said, sliding here naked leg between his thighs and kissing him.

***

"There you are," Joe Jimenez said, standing up and greeting Jesse and Grant with a hug at a table inside Bailey's Saloon.

Jesse reached in his jacket pocket and pulled out a plastic zip lock bag and handed it to Joe, saying, "Here's your father's property and our thanks."

"Did it do any good?" Joe asked.

"Yep, it sure did. We traced the residue back to a plastic explosive manufactured by a munitions plant in the Ukraine. That plant is owned by George Aristotle, a very bad man who we have since learned has gone to meet his maker," Jesse replied.

***

Snoopy and Grub sat snuggled on the love seat swing on the lanai of their rental beach cottage watching the sun set in Princeville, Kauai, Hawaii. It was their favorite island resort and they were delighted to share it as Mr. and Mrs. Tanaka.

Snoopy sighed and said, "That was such a great ceremony and I'm really glad we could share it with our friends."

"Yeah, and I have a question. When Dinosa toasted us and said 'here's to the virgin couple when they met', was that true about you?" Grub asked.

Snoops reached down inside his shorts, caressed his manhood and purred, "I'll never tell."

Would you like to see your manuscript become a book?

If you are interested in becoming a
PublishAmerica author, please submit your
manuscript for possible publication to us at:

acquisitions@publishamerica.com

You may also mail in your manuscript to:

**PublishAmerica
PO Box 151
Frederick, MD 21705**

We also offer free graphics for Children's Picture Books!

---

www.publishamerica.com

CPSIA information can be obtained at www.ICGtesting.com
Printed in the USA
BVOW07s2135190913

331654BV00001B/15/P